"WE'RE RIGHT IN THE MIDDLE OF A BALLOON BARRAGE!"
BOB SHOUTED.

Sky Attack   *Frontispiece (Page 60)*

SKY ATT

ACK

A LUCKY TERRELL FLYING STORY

SKY ATTACK

By

CANFIELD COOK

Illustrated by

FRANK DOBIAS

GROSSET & DUNLAP

Publishers   NEW YORK

CONTENTS

SKY ATTACK

SKY ATTACK

CHAPTER I

A Happy Reunion

"LUCKY" ROBERT TERRELL had been pacing up and and down the corridor, waiting to see the Senior Medical Officer who would give the all-important verdict. The minutes crept like hours. Just when Bob felt that he could contain his patience no longer, the door opened and an orderly spoke to him.

"You may come in now, Mr. Terrell."

Bob quickly entered the office.

"Flying Officer Terrell, sir," the orderly addressed the Senior Medical Officer.

"Good morning, Terrell. How do you feel?"

"Good morning, sir," replied Bob. "Why, I feel as if I——"

"Yes, yes, I think perhaps I know how you feel," interrupted the M.O. "You feel that if you don't get out of here soon and get back in the air, you'll blow up. Isn't that it?"

1

"That's just about right, sir," grinned Bob. "It's almost five months since I first entered the hospital and I'm feeling fit as a fiddle. In fact, sir, I'm quite sure I could have returned to the active list a long time ago."

"Yes, Terrell," agreed the M.O., "you could have climbed into your kite and given a pretty good account of yourself—for the first few minutes. After that you'd have been a sitting duck for any Jerry wanting to take a crack at you. Don't worry, you haven't been wasting your time and I don't think we've been wasting ours. Come here and let me take a look at you."

Nervous with anxiety Bob followed the Medical Officer into the examining room, fully aware of how much depended on this examination. Either he would be released or doomed to more time in the convalescent home.

"Sit down here, Terrell," directed the Medical Officer, and to the orderly who was standing near by, "Bring in Mr. Terrell's card, please."

"According to the records, Terrell," said the M.O., looking thoughtfully at the card, "you've had about five months hospitalization. Two weeks in France under the tender and, I might add, skillful auspices of the enemy, six weeks in the Southern General Hospital, and three months with us. That ought to be enough for anyone who had fractured his skull on French cobblestones and had been shot up by his own squadron mates when he flew back in a stolen Messerschmitt. What do you think?"

"I think it's more than enough," agreed Bob, surprised at the M.O.'s knowledge of his escape from France. "And if I may say so, sir, if I could fly back then, I ought to be able to fly now."

There was no immediate reply from the M.O. who was examining Bob's head and jaw. Apparently satisfied with what he saw, he instructed the still nervous Bob, "Get those trousers off now, Terrell, and climb up here on the table and I'll take a look at that leg of yours."

Bob removed his trousers as directed and stretched out on the examining table. There was still ample evidence of the damage done to his leg by the Spitfire bullets. Fortunately for Bob, Eric Prentiss had closed in so tightly when he attacked the supposed enemy that Bob had not received the full force of the eight-gun converging fire. Actually this fact had saved his leg, although the angry-looking scars bore testimony to the accuracy of his friend's marksmanship.

Very carefully the M.O. examined the injured leg, and Bob winced involuntarily as the doctor probed deeply. Try as he would, he could not help flinching.

"Don't let that worry you, Terrell," said the M.O. understandingly. "That wound will be tender for a long time to come, but I don't think it will interfere with your walking. It's the flying we have to worry about anyway."

"Oh, I'm not worrying about that," Bob assured him.

"Well, I am," responded the M.O. "While you've been in the hospital, ceilings have gone up a few thousand feet, which means even colder weather up on top. Let's check those reflexes now."

Bob slid off the table and sat in the chair with his knees crossed. With a small hard rubber hammer the M.O. tapped around his kneecap. Each time he hit a certain spot, Bob's leg jumped up—which was exactly what the M.O. wanted. Twenty minutes later the examination ended with a second check of the flier's blood pressure. The Medical Officer sat down at his desk and wrote the results on Bob's record card. Finally he turned to Bob.

"Well, Terrell, I think you'll do."

It was the long-awaited verdict. Bob Terrell heaved a deep sigh of relief and his tense nerves unkinked themselves, one by one.

"We've done all we can for you here," went on the M.O. "If you can pass the board this afternoon, you'll be ready for active duty again. The board will advise you where you'll be posted."

For a moment the thought of this second hurdle dampened Bob's jubilation. It had not occurred to him that he might be posted anywhere else than with his old Spitfire squadron under Squadron Leader Newcome.

"Come now, Terrell, buck up," urged the M.O., noting the disappointment in Bob's face. "I'm sure the board will pass you and, so far as I know, you'll be starting in again right where you left off. You will report to Room 415 at three this afternoon."

"Yes, sir," said Bob and, saluting smartly, he left the examining room.

Try as he would, Bob could not feel "bucked up."

It had been a long time since he had seen his squadron mates, and from all accounts they had been more than busy since he had been laid up. Slowly and thoughtfully he walked down the corridor toward the main entrance of the convalescent home.

"How did it go, Terrell?" inquired a bomber pilot wearing the arm band of a hospitalized service man on one sleeve, while the other was tucked in his tunic belt.

Bob told him what had happened and also of his fears regarding the coming examination by the medical board.

"If old Eagle Eye has passed you, you've nothing more to worry about," his friend cheerfully assured him.

Suddenly Bob felt very much ashamed. Here was a wounded pilot who could count on nothing better than discharge from the service, and yet he was taking the trouble to cheer him—Bob Terrell—whose only worry was how soon he could start flying again.

As Bob walked on he saw many others who would never again feel the thrill of being "on top." The very sight of them gave him a better appreciation of his own good fortune.

"Hi, there, Lucky!" came a familiar voice as Bob walked out on the lawn.

"Eric!" exclaimed the delighted Bob. "Gosh, but I'm glad to see you."

They pumped each other's hands as if it had been years instead of months since they had last been together.

"Wait a minute there, Prentiss, you can't have all Bob's attention. I'm here, too." It was Don White who spoke.

"Well, Don!" Bob's joy at seeing his two buddies was obvious. "This is really great. How in the world did you two happen to get down here?"

"Well, Bob," began Eric, "we heard that they might be letting you out soon, so we thought we'd better get down here before you were wished back on the squadron. Squadron Leader Newcome gave us a forty-eight-hour leave, and he ordered us to see to it that you are kept here." Eric paused for dramatic effect before he added, "That is, of course, unless you can come back with us."

"You mean Newcome really wants me back?"

"Of course he does," broke in Don. "We're down here to bring home that Texas bacon, though why anybody would want Texas bacon when Canadian is available, I'm sure I don't know."

"The way I feel right now I don't even mind your Canuck wisecracks, Don, and as for Eric's reverse English—well, I'm glad to hear that, too. I've certainly been anxious to see you fellows. I've had so little word from the squadron that I was beginning to think that Newcome might not be taking me back and that I'd be posted somewhere else. After all these months in the hospital that would have been the last straw. Let's go on up to my room where we can do some real 'bunk flying.'"

As Bob led the way his two friends seemed to be lagging behind and he caught the whispered words, "Maybe we shouldn't tell him."

"Shouldn't tell him what?" asked Bob as soon as they were in his room.

"Oh, it's really nothing, Bob," answered the embarrassed Don, "only of course you know that after five months there are bound to be a lot of changes in an operational fighter squadron. We're afraid that it won't seem the same to you at all. Among other things, there have been a number of replacements. Blackwell was posted missing a few days ago.

In fact, there aren't many of the old crowd left."

"I sort of expected that," replied Bob soberly.

Don went on to tell about Blackwell, but Bob knew there was something else—something really important—they were keeping from him. Better let them bring it out in their own way, he decided, while aloud he said, "Believe it or not, I've reached the point where I'd be willing to pilot bombers so long as it got me back in active service."

"You'd what?" asked the surprised Eric. "I seem to remember your saying once upon a time that piloting bombers was little better than driving a lorry."

"Yes, I know, and I still feel that way," admitted Bob, "but rather than stay on here, I'd . . ."

"You would?" interrupted Eric. "All right, young man, you may get a chance to do exactly that."

"Exactly what?" asked the completely puzzled Bob.

"Better tell him the whole thing from the beginning, Eric," advised Don White.

"All right," said Eric, "here goes. We all know that the R.A.F. is carrying the air war to the Nazis at a faster and heavier pace all the time. Last year we were getting it in the neck from the Luftwaffe. Now the Jerries are so busy on the eastern front against Russia that they haven't enough bombers to go around. Even if they had, our fighter defense has become so much stronger than it was during the last blitzes that we're better able to take care of ourselves. Right now is our opportunity to get in some real blasting on Germany. It may be enough to stop the war entirely if we can get at their war industries. Do you follow me?"

"Sure, I follow you. Go on."

"Well, that's where we come in," continued Eric. "The Bomber Command has to draw on all the experienced pilots they can find to fly a new type of high. altitude bomber. It not only flies high and fast, but it also carries a heavy bomb load. With it the Bomber Command thinks we can give an added punch to the job the boys have been doing in the Wellingtons and Whitleys, the Hamptons and Blenheims. Squadron Leader Newcome has been asked to recommend three pilots from his squadron to tackle it. He spoke to Don and me about it and we've decided to go. We asked him if you could go with us. He says it's all right with him if it is with you. How about it, Bob?"

"How about it? What do you mean, 'how about it?'" demanded the eager Bob. "Look out, Fritz, here we come!"

CHAPTER II

Action Over the Channel

THE early morning channel patrol already had cleared the airdrome when Bob, Eric Prentiss, and Don White clumped down toward the hangar line. In spite of the cumbersome awkwardness of the heavy flying suit, the "Mae West" life belt, and the parachute which kept banging behind, Bob could not help feeling a sense of keen excitement. On the camouflaged green asphalt tarmac in front of B Hangar stood three Spitfires, their propellers ticking over idly. These were the aircraft to be flown to Littlesgate for engine replacements.

"Good morning, sir." The Flight Sergeant saluted Bob smartly as he approached his assigned aircraft. "Everything is O.K., sir, filled up with petrol and ammunition. I hope you have a nice trip, sir."

"Thank you," said Bob, returning the salute. "I won't be looking for much excitement on this trip, but the simplest kind of flying will seem exciting after all these months on the ground."

"Good luck, anyway, and if you see any Jerries on the way give them my regards, will you, sir?"

"I'll do that little thing," promised Bob with a grin.

Eric Prentiss, as Senior Flying Officer, was in charge of the section of three planes. Releasing his brakes and gunning his engine, he taxied out to one end of the runway. Don and Bob followed suit.

"O.K., Mr. Prentiss," Bob heard through the R.T. system, and in another second Eric's plane was roaring down the runway. Next came the clearance for Don and his plane roared on after Eric's.

Bob, trembling with excitement, waited for his own clearance. He wondered what it would feel like, this first flight in the Spitfire after such a long period on the ground. There was little time to speculate, however, for the next second came the O.K. Giving her the gun, Bob was off, and as his tail lifted and the wheels left the ground, all sense of strangeness disappeared. As he tucked up his undercarriage and climbed after his two friends, nervous excitement gave way to a glorious feeling of exhilaration. At five thousand feet Bob overhauled the other two and dropped into his assigned position just behind Eric's port wing, with Don White flying the other trailing edge of the "V." White was formating quite tightly, so Bob followed suit.

"How do you feel, Bob?" called out Eric over the R.T.

"Never better," answered Bob. "This is certainly the life!"

"Maybe we'd better slow down a bit for him," interjected Don. "After all, we mustn't forget that he's still an invalid."

"Wait until I get you on the ground, Don," promised Bob, "I'll show you how much of an invalid I am."

"He's certainly not flying like an invalid," commented Eric. "Bob, you've been pushing me for the last five minutes. How about easing up a bit, and taking that starboard wing of yours out of my lap. What do you want me to do, scratch it for you?"

"O.K.," said Bob, inching back on the throttle. "If that's the kind of flying you fellows have been doing while I've been away, I suppose I'll have to hold back, although I had thought you were real Spitfire pilots."

"I think we'd better cut out the conversation, fellows," said Eric. "After all, we don't know when a call may be coming in over the R.T. Let's ease up over this cloud bank and keep our eyes open. Who knows, we may have some fun on this ferry trip."

At eleven thousand feet they leveled off, forging ahead eastward into the morning sun. As they sped along, Bob kept a wary eye on his rear-vision mirror and over his port wing. Don White would be taking care of the starboard side and Eric would be watching for anything that might be coming at them out of the sun.

Bob now felt perfectly at home in his Spitfire. It fitted him like an old glove. It seemed as though his last flight had been yesterday instead of several months ago. Although thrilled to think of the adventures that lay ahead, he hated to leave Y Squadron. And he especially hated to leave Squadron Leader Newcome. After piloting the Spitfires to Littlesgate, Don, Eric and Bob were to report to the Bomber Command in London, where they would fly a new type of bomber—the last word in fighting aircraft.

The three Spitfires bored on through the sky.

They had it all to themselves; there was no sign of a plane anywhere in the blue. Up in front the old Merlin purred along rhythmically. Bob did not think that it sounded much like an engine in need of replacement, but his musings were cut short as their call letters came crackling in over the R.T. system.

"OXY, what is your altitude? OXY, what is your altitude?"

Quickly Eric responded, "OXY altitude eleven thousand. OXY altitude eleven thousand."

"Stand by for changed orders. Stand by for changed orders," came back the command.

The three pilots sat tensely in their Spitfires wondering what was coming. Bob, especially, after his enforced idleness, hoped that it meant action.

Then came the instructions from the Group Fighter Command. He reported that two German battleships and a cruiser had escaped from their berths on the French coast and were making a desperate dash for the Channel, in the hope of reaching the North Sea and the greater safety of a German port farther removed from British bombing attacks. The three Spitfires were to act as a roving unit and engage any enemy fighters that might be protecting the escape of the battleships.

Eric Prentiss curtly acknowledged the orders. "O.K., fellows, you've heard it. Looks like big business," he called to Bob and Don. Easing the Spitfire's nose down, he tore through the clouds.

Bob was astounded at the audacity of the Nazi plan. He knew that for many months the Bomber Command had been pounding away at the German warships berthed in the French port. How could they ever hope to escape? Why had they attempted it? He knew that in their dash up the rapidly narrowing channel they would soon come to a point where only twenty miles of water separated the French and English coasts. At that point they would come within range of British land-based guns, to say nothing of the bombers flying above them.

The flying was getting ticklish now, for their speed had been greatly increased by the dive down through the clouds. Bob hung on grimly as the altimeter unwound rapidly toward zero. For an invalid this was excitement with a vengeance. Desperately, Bob tried to hold his position as he plunged after Eric, but only a portion of Eric's plane was visible at any time—now a wing tip, now the tail. At less than a thousand feet, Eric leveled off beneath the cloud layers. Down below, the shore line was clearly visible. They were headed almost due east, but visibility was limited to a few miles.

"The first thing we've got to do is find them," called out Eric over the R.T., "and that's going to be some job, because it's thickening up all the time."

Taking into consideration their time in the air and their air speed, Bob estimated that at this particular point the Channel would be approximately seventy miles wide. If so, it would take about six minutes to reach the center, and in another five they would be over the French coast. From the position given by the Group Fighter Command, the escaping cruisers were even nearer the narrow part of the Channel.

Eric now banked slightly to starboard and led his section in a southeasterly direction. This course should bring them somewhere in the battle area within the next quarter hour. Bob searched sky and sea, but saw no sign of action anywhere.

Soon they were flying at a height of somewhat under five hundred feet, and in the Channel below Bob could see a small trawler, probably a mine sweeper, plying its way undisturbed toward the English coast. In just a few seconds the coast was no longer visible because of lowering clouds. The Jerries certainly had been smart to get their cruisers up the Channel under this low cloud ceiling which made bombing impossible from any height. Any air attacks would have to be made by torpedo planes or dive bombers. All that the Spitfires could do would be to protect their attack.

Eric stepped up the speed of his plane and then suddenly his voice came over the R.T. "Keep an eye on those rear-vision mirrors. It's hard to tell what we'll run into. Above all, watch your petrol gauges, for we can't afford to be caught short out here."

Still there was no sign of enemy planes or the Jerry battleships.

"There they are, Eric, to starboard!" called Don White excitedly over the R.T.

In the distance Bob could see three vague shadows on the water.

"O.K., fellows," said Eric. "Looks like it will have to be every man for himself. Try to cover our fellows when they attack. Don't forget we've got a date in Littlesgate and then London."

With that, Eric pulled up into the clouds and disappeared. Don banked sharply to starboard and also disappeared into the clouds. Bob was alone.

"Well, I like that," Bob mumbled to himself, although he realized the wisdom of breaking up. There was no point in presenting a large target for the guns of those battleships, which could do plenty of damage when they got going.

In the seconds that folllowed the disappearance of Don and Eric, Bob had drawn close enough to the warships to see white bow waves foaming out in front of each, while boiling wakes trailed behind. He estimated their speed to be at least thirty knots. Heavy smoke poured from the funnels of the battleships and effectively concealed their turrets, but even as he watched, Bob saw great flashes of red fire pour from the port side of the nearest battleship. Never before had he felt so impotent. What could a Spitfire with its eight machine guns do against a steelclad battleship?

Then suddenly Bob saw what the Nazis were firing at. Low, almost on the surface of the Channel, torpedo planes of the Fleet Air Arm were launching an attack, coming in toward their quarry on an oblique line. They were now banking toward him, and Bob could see silvery shafts cut through the water in the direction of their target. In a desperate attempt to avoid the coming torpedoes, the warships had changed their course.

Forgetting his own danger, Bob shoved his nose down so as to see the results more clearly, but the acrid smoke screen enveloped him. His own plane was tossed roughly by the shock of the tremendous explosion and for a moment was out of control. Clear of the smoke, he found himself headed straight down into the Channel. With only inches to spare, he finally managed to pull out over the wave tops.

Twisting and turning aircraft were all around him. There was no time now to watch the warships. Out of the corner of his eye Bob could see dive bombers going into the attack. The slow-moving torpedo planes were trying desperately to get back to shore, but Bob could see only about half the number that had been in the fight originally. ME 109's and 110's were attacking them from all sides.

Seeing his opportunity, Bob boosted his engine and made after an ME 110. One of his own wing tips crumpled under the Nazi cannon fire, but he kept on going. A few seconds later the Jerry plane was in his range. Squeezing the button, he could feel the Spitter's lethal stream of lead spew from his eight machine guns. He held the button until flame and smoke burst from the Nazi warplane as it plummeted down into the Channel.

"That's one gone," Bob said aloud. But his elation was cut short when he felt the impact of bullets against his Spitfire. He banked sharply as an ME 109 rocketed by. This was the closest air fighting Bob had ever seen. A five-hundred-foot ceiling meant that the action was practically on the water.

The tail gunners in the torpedo planes were making a valiant effort to beat off the Jerries, and Bob wondered why the planes did not pull up into the clouds for a getaway. Then he noticed that the torpedo planes were so badly shot up they were unable to climb. Indeed they were fortunate in being able to keep above water. Ahead, a fog was closing in on the Channel and if they made the fog, they would be safe.

While taking in the situation, Bob had recovered from his dive on the ME 110 and had pulled around for another run on the attacking Jerry. As he zoomed up, a 109 came into his sights, but even as he pressed the button, it slithered off. A sharp-shooting torpedo plane gunner had beaten him to the draw. Quickly Bob banked to starboard to avoid colliding with the falling plane. As he did so, he again felt the impact of bullets against his Spitter, and in the rear-vision mirror he saw a 110 right on his tail. Fortunately, the Nazi's cannon shots were wide and only the machine-gun bullets struck him. He could see the gashes in the wing just beside the fuselage. Sideslipping to port, away from the gun-fire, Bob would have sworn that the tip of his prop touched the waves as he pulled up in a tight-climbing turn to get beneath his opponent's tail.

The Nazi, unable to execute this tight maneuver, started to hare off after an easier victim, one of the torpedo planes. The belly of the ship was in Bob's range as he climbed. Squeezing the button, his bullets cut a deep gash in the ME's fuselage. Ruddering slightly, he watched his next burst cut through the port wing at the fuselage. Still squeezing the button, he saw the wing flung clear, while the rest of the plane shot seaward, narrowly missing the torpedo plane it had been attacking. Only by quick maneuvering was Bob able to dodge the falling wing.

"Well, that's number two," he thought. "Not bad work for a fellow just out of the hospital." Glancing quickly at the fuel gauge, he saw that there was still plenty of petrol. If the fog closed in, however, there would be little chance of further action. There was no aircraft in sight now, so Bob decided to find the enemy warships. They must not be allowed to escape. Not that one lone Spitfire could stop them, but there was plenty of ammunition in the Spitter to make it unhealthy for the deck gunners.

Checking with his compass, he pulled around again to the southeast, confident that the warships had not gotten very far away in the few minutes he had been tied up with the Jerries. With full-out engine, he pulled through the thickening mist and in a few moments caught the fumes of the smoke screen. Dropping down as low as he dared, Bob could see the boiling wake of the warships. One dark bulk loomed up almost directly ahead of him. Yanking back on the stick, he missed the super-structure by inches.

That was a bit too close, so he decided to figure things out a little more carefully. Leveling off at a thousand feet, he saw the two battleships and the cruiser directly below him, forging ahead with undiminished speed. Banking around to run in from the stern, he saw several blurred shapes darting toward the battleships. They were dive bombers of the Fleet Air Arm, and as they dived, fire streamed from the warships' decks. Bob could feel the shells whishing by as his Spitfire was buffeted around like a leaf in the wind. Then the dive bombers flattened out, one of them falling in flames toward the deck of the port warship. At the same instant the farther battleship was enveloped in a mass of flame and billowing smoke. Some of the bombs had struck home.

The whole scene was now enshrouded in smoke from the explosion, and Bob could not be sure how successful the dive bombers had been. There was still enough visibility, however, for a diving attack on one of the warships. Bob decided to try it. As he dropped closer to the level of the water, the smoke cleared and the battleships were again silhouetted against the haze. So far as he could tell, most of the anti-aircraft fire was coming from the after-deck where there was no superstructure to interfere with his dive and getaway. If he tried it forward, he might become entangled with the mast. Now the ship's gunners had seen him and were concentrating their attention on his plane. Whatever the damage by the dive bombers, it had not stopped the anti-aircraft fire.

Rolling over, Bob pointed the nose of his Spitfire for the afterdeck of the port battleship. If he could clear it and get into the fog, he'd be safe. Down he plunged, the old Merlin screaming. Shafts of light streamed toward him, and he sensed rather than felt the hits on his plane.

Now he could see the gunners on the deck. Squeezing the button tightly, he concentrated on a group of gunners near the stern and a moment later their fire ceased. He could see his bullets move swiftly along the deck toward another gun emplacement, while white-faced men fell sprawling on the steel deck as the Spitfire screamed by.

For an instant Bob thought he had judged the pull-out too closely, and as he plunged on through the fog, he feared that at any moment he would feel the impact of the water. Nobly recovering, the Spitfire shot skywards. Leveling off, Bob took stock of the damage.

It was difficult to see anything, for the fog was streaming by in a moisture-laden mass over the fuselage and wings. The Spitter was heavier on the controls and the right wing dropped sharply. Quickly Bob checked his instruments and with horror noted the fuel gauge. When he had last looked, it was half full. Now he doubted that there was enough for him to reach shore. One of the petrol tanks must have been hit, and if it had, there was not only the possibility of running out of fuel, but also the danger of fire breaking out at any moment. Aware that the cockpit was filling with the odor of petrol, Bob climbed for more altitude in case a jump would be necessary. Soon he left the fog behind and broke out in the clear at approximately two thousand feet.

Now he could survey the full damage done by the battleship's guns. The right wing tip had been completely shot away and a gaping hole appeared midway between the fuselage and the point where the wing tip should have been. The left wing was also pockmarked from the battleship's fire. What a fool he had been to tackle a battleship with a Spitfire! The more he thought about it, the more he realized that it was sheer luck that had brought him through. He certainly would be in a tough spot now if any Nazi planes hove in sight.

Suddenly in the rear-vision mirror Bob saw what appeared to be a whole squadron of aircraft on his tail. As he nosed down to the friendly clouds, one detached itself and made straight for him. Wondering whether or not his starboard wing would hang together in the dive, Bob saw the pursuing aircraft bank away, revealing the tricolored rondels of the Royal Air Force on the underside of the wing.

Thankfully, Bob flattened out, cutting down his speed to the lowest possible cruising tempo. This was more good luck, for these chaps would be headed for the coast and he could follow them in. In a moment, a squadron of Hurricanes was overhead and Bob gunned his ship to keep up with them.

"O.K., Spitter," came the cheery voice of the Squadron Leader over the R.T. "Follow us. When we drop down to cloud level, you keep right on going underneath. You'll find an airdrome there.

In the meantime, it might be a good idea to stick your thumb in that wing hole of yours."

"Much obliged," replied Bob, tailing the Hurricane. While he hardly could appreciate the Squadron Leader's humor, he certainly was glad they had come along. His fuel gauge was now alarmingly near zero. Since he had started out to ferry the Spitfire to Littlesgate, he would like to get it down one way or another, even if it meant a crash landing. His air speed was now so low that when the Hurricanes dropped into the clouds they were almost a mile ahead of him.

Continuing to the point where he thought they had disappeared, Bob eased back on the throttle and dropped down gently through the clouds. At five hundred feet he emerged in the clear above the English countryside. There was no fog, but where was the airdrome? His eyes searched the ground and over the port wing he saw three aircraft taking off from a level space. As he banked around to level off for a landing, the Merlin sputtered and died.

The field was almost directly underneath now, and with a little more luck he would make it. Five hundred feet left little room for a turn on a dead stick, but in a moment he was around and headed for the runway. Fishtailing desperately, he missed the paved strip, and his right wing dropped dangerously. Recovering in the nick of time, Bob felt his wheels bite the rough turf. Instinctively he'd lowered them on the way down through the clouds.

CHAPTER III

FURTHER ORDERS

Bob pulled back the greenhouse casing as a tractor sped toward him across the airdrome. One of the two aircraftmen leaped out of the tractor and came over to the plane.

"It looks as if the mice have been nibbling at you, sir."

"That's right," agreed Bob. "About thirty thousand tons each."

"Oh, were you in on that show?" inquired the man eagerly.

"Not very much of it," admitted Bob. "I don't know whether I was in at the tail end or the beginning. But I do know one thing: I'm darn glad to be here."

The aircraftman hitched the tractor to the tail of Bob's Spitfire and hauled it onto the tarmac in front of the hangar. Bob climbed stiffly out of the cramped cockpit and he and the Flight Sergeant inspected the damaged plane.

31

"What do you think, Flight? Will I be able to take off all right? I'm anxious to get on up to Littlesgate."

"Well, sir," said the Flight Sergeant. "I think you were lucky to get in here, let alone to Littlesgate. But if you'll give me half an hour to check the plane while you're reporting in at Operations, then I'll let you know whether or not you can go on."

When Bob saw the full extent of the damage—wings and fuselage peppered with shrapnel, and a hole in the starboard wing large enough to jump through—he was amazed that he had escaped with his skin.

"By the way," asked Bob, "how far is it to Littlesgate?"

"I don't rightly know, sir," replied the aircraftman, "but I believe it's about fifty miles. Excuse me, sir," he added, "but haven't you been here before?"

"Here before?" repeated Bob, puzzled. "No, I don't believe so."

"I could have sworn I'd seen you here before, sir."

"There *is* something familiar about this place," thought Bob as he trudged over to the dispersal hut.

Entering, he found it deserted, except for a Briefing Officer seated at a desk in one corner.

"I'm Flying Officer Terrell, sir," Bob introduced himself. "I've just made a forced landing on your field."

"Well, Terrell," replied the Intelligence Officer, "glad to know you and happy you made the landing all right. What happened?"

"I'm not too sure myself," replied Terrell. "All I know is that three of us started off from Y Squadron down the coast towards Littlesgate, ferrying three Spitfires for engine replacements. We'd been airborne only half an hour when orders came in over the R.T. for us to lend a hand in this battleship show."

"I see," said the Intelligence Officer with interest. "Tell me what happened. All our kites are up in that show, too, and I'm anxiously awaiting some word."

Bob told him what he could of his experience. "I don't mind saying, sir," he added, "that I felt pretty much like a duck out of water. The ceiling was so low there wasn't much I could do."

"It sounds to me as if you'd done quite a bit, Terrell," said the Intelligence Officer. "Probably most of our fighter aircraft were busy up above the overcast and that's why you didn't see them. There ought to be further word any minute now. There it is!" he added as the loud-speaker began to crackle.

Bob listened to the report that came from Squadron Leader Stanton.

"Why, I know Stanton!" he exclaimed.

"You'll be seeing him very soon," said the Intelligence Officer. "He's our Commanding Officer here."

Now Bob understood why the station had looked so familiar. It was here that he had made a forced landing several months before, and he recalled how well Squadron Leader Stanton had treated him then.

"I seem to be making a habit of this," said Bob, going on to tell the Intelligence Officer about his previous visit.

"I've been trying to place you, Terrell, and now that explains it all. We're glad to have you here. After all, that's what airdromes are for—forced landings, if necessary. Why don't you take off those duds and make yourself comfortable until Squadron Leader Stanton gets back."

"Thanks," said Bob, "but I believe I'll walk down to the tarmac instead and see how they're getting along with my Spitter. I'm anxious to get on to Littlesgate if it's possible to make the kite airworthy."

"I'm afraid it will take two or three hours to fix you up for the air again," said the Flight Sergeant when Bob came up to inquire about his plane. "And only well enough to get you to Littlesgate," he added.

"That's good enough for me," replied Bob, "so long as I can make it before dark. By the way, Flight, you were perfectly right in saying that you thought you recognized me. I have been here before, but I didn't realize it until I reached the dispersal hut. I was the fellow who nearly mowed you all down when I came in for a forced landing several months back."

"There they come now, sir," interjected the Flight Sergeant. "And it looks like we've copped it rather badly. There were twelve went out, sir."

Bob watched the nine Hurricanes come in one by one for the landing and then taxi on up to the tarmac. Squadron Leader Stanton looked grim when he alighted from his plane a few moments later. Gone was that infectious cheeriness that Bob remembered from his first meeting. His aircraft was marked up almost as badly as Bob's. The others also bore marks of recent combat.

"Well, Terrell," the C.O. greeted him, "so you're back to see us again."

"Yes, sir," replied Bob, "I'm here again."

"That your kite, Terrell?" asked the C.O., pointing to the Spitfire now being hauled into the hangar.

"Yes, sir, what there is left of it. Tell me, sir," he inquired anxiously, "did they get away? The battleships, I mean."

"Oh, were you in that show, Terrell? If you were, you may know more about it than I do, for we didn't see hide nor hair of the battleships. Our instructions were to engage enemy fighters above the overcast, and consequently we saw nothing that went on below. Did you?"

Terrell told him what he could, going on to explain that he was on his way to the Bomber Command in London to report for transfer.

"That being the case, Terrell," replied the C.O., "you'd better make out a complete report here with

our Intelligence and we can relay it to your Squadron. Let's go back to the dispersal hut, and after
briefing, we'll have lunch together."

After making out a detailed operations report, Bob
handed it to the Briefing Officer.

"Thanks, Terrell," he said. "Your account of that
torpedo attack should be valuable, and if any of
those torpedo planes reach shore, we may be able to
confirm your victory."

Bob was glad when lunch was over, for a pilot's
mess is not a cheerful place right after three of their
group have been lost. A spirit of deep gloom over-
hung the whole station because, as fighter pilots,
there was little they could do about the escape of
the warships, and Bob's report only deepened the
conviction that they had gotten away.

"Here's hoping you have a forced landing here in
one of those new jobs you're going to fly," said
Stanton when Bob was ready to leave. "I'd certainly like to examine one of those bombers. But
take my tip and don't start strafing any more battleship decks with a Spitfire. They weren't built for
that."

"Right, sir," smiled Bob. "I'm hoping that in the

future I'll be carrying a better prescription for them."

When he reached the tarmac Bob was amazed at the transformation in his Spitfire. The large hole in the right wing had been covered over. The petrol tanks had not been damaged, but a break found in one of the petrol lines accounted for the loss of fuel. The Merlin already was warmed up when Bob arrived, ready for the take-off. Thanking the Flight Sergeant for his trouble, he taxied out to the end of the runway and awaited the clearance signal.

Soon he was on his way, and fifteen minutes later his wheels were settling down on the runway at Littlesgate. Bob had not had much time to think about Eric and Don since his tangle with the battleships, but he was greatly relieved to find them awaiting him on the tarmac. They waved gaily as he taxied in.

"Gosh!" exclaimed Don, "it looks as if the moths had been at you, too."

"They called 'em mice over at the Hurricane Squadron," laughed Bob.

"It's mighty good to see you, Bob," said Eric. "We wondered what had happened to you. Do you know what happened to the battleships?"

It was soon evident that Bob had more news than either Don or Eric. Having lost the battleships, they had climbed up on top and tackled the Jerry fighters. Neither could be as sure of his victories as Bob was, for their adversaries had dropped out of control into the clouds.

"We'll have to do a lot of explaining to Squadron Leader Newcome," said Eric. "We were supposed to bring up three Spitfires for engine replacements and it looks as if they'll have to replace three entire airplanes."

"Come on, Bob," urged Don. "Get a move on. Eric has arranged for a car to take us to London."

In a little over an hour, the R.A.F. car was nosing its way through the dense traffic in the Strand and a few minutes later it pulled up in front of the main entrance to the Royal Air Force Headquarters.

"We're to report to the Fighter Command first," said Eric.

After the guide had escorted them through a maze of offices to the Fighter Command, Eric acted as spokesman for the three.

"We are reporting from Y Squadron for transfer," Eric told the orderly.

"Please be seated, gentlemen," he replied.

After waiting ten minutes they were escorted into a private office where a high ranking officer of the Royal Air Force was seated at a large desk in the center of the room. The three pilots stood stiffly at attention.

"Please be seated," said the Air Commodore, after shaking hands. "What I have to say won't take long. You three from Y Squadron, along with many others from other squadrons, have been chosen on the recommendation of your individual Squadron Commanders for a very special job. From your records and recommendations, we believe you have the peculiar adaptability required."

The boys listened in silence, for no reply seemed necessary.

"You will be transferred to the Bomber Command to fly a new type of aircraft," the Air Commodore went on. "Tomorrow morning at nine o'clock you are to report to the Littlesgate Airdrome. There you will receive further instructions. Is everything clear?"

"Why, yes, sir," replied Eric hesitantly. "Only we understood that we'd be going up north."

"That is correct," said the Air Commodore, "but as long as you are attached to the Fighter Command, we're going to make as much use of you as possible. This time you will be ferrying a new type of aircraft up to Scotland. You should be at your destination within an hour after leaving Littlesgate. Incidentally," he added slyly, "I hope your ships arrive in better shape than those you just took in to Littlesgate."

"But you see, sir," broke in Eric.

"Yes, I understand," replied the Air Commodore, smiling. "I've had complete reports on today's show and they indicate that you fellows have given a pretty good account of yourselves. Now the orderly will check you in at the Bomber Command. And good luck to you."

"We don't know much more than we did before," said Bob when they had left the Air Commodore's office, "but at least we'll have a chance to fly the new fighters, and that's something."

"Something!" said Eric. "I'll say it's something. The Air Commodore said we'd be there in something less than an hour; that is, from Littlesgate to the field in Scotland. Do you fellows realize that must be over three hundred and fifty miles?"

"If we have any more detours like today's fracas, it'll take more than an hour," said Bob.

The interview with the Bomber Command was even briefer than that at the Fighter Command. The three pilots were told simply to report to R.A.F. Headquarters in Edinburgh, and that transportation was being provided for them.

"But, sir," said Eric, "transportation is already arranged for. We're flying some new fighters up to Scotland."

"That's fine," said the Administrative Officer.

"Could you tell us where we'll be stationed, sir, or anything about the new bomber we're to fly?" asked Bob, always curious.

"Sorry, Terrell," replied the Administrative Officer, "everything about this new aircraft and the training base is strictly secret. Confidentially, however, and quite unofficially, I might say that you'll be flying the hottest thing in the air."

"Little by little, we'll get the story," said Bob as they left the office. "Tomorrow we fly a hot fighter, then we fly a hot bomber. Who could ask for more?"

"Right now," said Don, "the thought of some hot food interests me more than anything else."

"That's a good idea," agreed Eric. "We'll have a spot of tea."

"A spot of tea!" said Bob scornfully. "I'm all set for a regular meal. Now down in Texas where I come from we don't eat as often as you do, but when we do, oh, boy!"

"That's the way it is in Canada, too," agreed Don. "The trouble with you English is that you eat too much between meals and spoil your appetites."

"Don't worry about that," Eric assured him, "whenever you find me without an appetite, you'll know there's something really wrong."

"Say, fellows," said Bob, stopping suddenly on the sidewalk outside of headquarters, "do you realize that we'll likely be in Edinburgh before our baggage arrives in London? We'd better hop over to Waterloo and check up on that right away. Otherwise we'll have shopping to do."

"By jove, that's right," said Eric, hailing a taxi.

The three boys jumped in and a few minutes later were speeding over Waterloo Bridge on their way to the station.

"There's one thing I can't get used to," said Don.

"What's that?" queried Eric.

"This keeping to the left side of the road. I'm certainly glad it doesn't apply in the air."

"Look, fellows," said Bob, pointing to the Houses of Parliament, "there's a sight for you."

"And look at that balloon barrage around them," commented Eric. "I'd hate to have to thread my way through that, even in daylight."

At the station Bob's fears were proved groundless, for their luggage had arrived. Having been assured it would arrive in Edinburgh on the following morning, they re-directed it to R.A.F. Headquarters there.

"Now that that's over," said Don, "let's find a hotel and then let's eat."

It was some time before the boys found room enough for the three of them, and then it turned out to be one large room with three cots.

"At least we're all together," said Bob, "but I can't say much for English hotels."

"Not even the English say much for them," agreed Eric, "but with a war on, we're lucky to get anything."

"How about taking in a good show after dinner?" suggested Bob. "It may be our last chance for a long while."

"Good idea," agreed Eric.

"I'm for it," said Don, "but let's hurry up and get that food. I'm starved."

"I know just the place for you, Don," said Eric.

In spite of strict rationing, the food was both good and plentiful at the spot Eric had chosen. Except for the number of men in uniform, one would not have realized that the country was at war.

At an adjoining table four men in civilian clothes were carrying on a low-voiced conversation. Bob gathered, from the snatches he could not help overhearing, that they were engaged in armament manufacture, for their talk was all about some kind of switch that was actuated by temperature.

"We'll have to hurry," Eric said urgently, "if we're going to take in a show. It's almost eight o'clock now."

"After that meal," protested Don, "I don't want to walk too fast."

"After what you ate, Don," teased Bob, "you'll be

lucky to find a theater with a seat large enough to hold you. Goodness knows how you'll get into the cockpit tomorrow morning."

"I notice you didn't do so badly for an invalid, Bob."

After much discussion, the boys decided to see a musical comedy that had come over recently from the States. Although Bob thoroughly enjoyed the show, for some reason he could not forget the four men he had noticed in the restaurant. Later, he was to regret that he had not tried to hear more of their conversation.

CHAPTER IV

WHEN SPITFIRE MEETS STUKA

ENGLISH trains always intrigued Bob. Unlike American trains, with aisles running down the center of the car and seats on either side, the English cars usually had an aisle on one side which opened into compartments large enough for eight people. It was a very cozy way to travel, Bob decided. The train they took to Littlesgate, however, had no aisle at all. Instead, each compartment had two doors— one on either side of the train.

"I can't get used to these English trains," he told Eric. "We don't have anything like them at home."

"You see, Bob," explained Eric, "our distances are much shorter than they are in America. Consequently, our coaches are much lighter, although I think you'll agree they are just as comfortable and the trains travel just as fast or even faster."

When the train rolled to a stop at Littlesgate a short time later, the boys scrambled out. A waiting Royal Air Force tender whisked them out to the

field, and soon they were closeted with the Com.
manding Officer.

"Now remember, you chaps," said the C.O.,
"these Spitters have to be delivered in Edinburgh,
where they are badly needed. So don't take any
chances on the way. Although you haven't flown
this new type before I don't think you'll have any
trouble. Just remember that now you have a lot
more horses up there in front, so it's easy on the controls. And," he added significantly, "if you should
need to use your guns, there's a little surprise in
store for you. Now if you'll report to Flight Lieutenant Cameron, Commanding Number One Flight,
he will show you the ropes and start you off."

The three pilots hurried to Number One Flight,
eager to fly one of the new Spitfire types, equipped
with either twelve machine guns or a combination
of machine guns and cannon. Both types had a far
more powerful Merlin engine than anything they
had flown yet.

Flight Lieutenant Cameron proved to be a friendly
chap. He explained the differences between the new
type and the ones they had been used to.

"There's really nothing to it, fellows. It's just a

case of 'easy does it.' Go light on the controls and don't try standing them on their tails until you're off the ground at least. Remember, we want these Spitters to arrive in Edinburgh in one piece and not in the condition of those kites you brought in here yesterday."

The boys grinned assent. Each was itching to get into the cockpit of this new ship. As they approached the planes on the tarmac, Bob noticed the two long muzzles sticking out from the wings— one on either side of the fuselage. Those were cannon. He could not help hoping there would be an opportunity to see their devastating effects.

Flight Lieutenant Cameron quickly familiarized them with the cockpit, where there were only a few minor changes in instruments.

"I think that's all, fellows," said the Flight Lieutenant when he had shown them everything new. "We might as well go over to the dispersal hut now while the aircraftmen are warming up the engines."

There, with the Briefing Officer, a flight plan was worked out. Weather reports were good, with a high overcast predicted for the entire distance. That was just fine for Bob who wanted to see the country-

side. All too frequently the limited visibility pre-
vented it.

Eric, as senior ranking officer, was again in charge
of the flight. He instructed Bob and Don to fly in
their accustomed positions. According to the flight
plan they would fly over some of the most heavily
industrialized sections of England, which would
necessitate detours to avoid balloon barrages. Fortunately for Bob's sight-seeing ideas a low flight level
was assigned.

Retrieving their parachutes and flying togs the
boys were soon ready for the air.

"Good luck, fellows," said Flight Lieutenant
Cameron cheerily as they walked over to the waiting Spitfires, "and don't forget those check points
and the balloon barrages. Remember, these ships
must arrive."

Bob fed the engine gingerly as he taxied over to
the runway. Even before gunning his engine for
the take-off, he could sense the tremendous power
of the new Merlin. Roaring down the runway, he
was airborne in seconds and soon joined Eric and
Don.

This plane gave him the same sense of power that

he had felt on escaping from France in the captured Messerschmitt.   A Spitfire like this would be a worthy opponent for the powerful German aircraft. The air-speed indicator passed the three hundred mile an hour mark while they still were climbing, and the engine had plenty of power in reserve.   As there was no ban on the use of the radiotelephone, Bob called to Eric.

"I wish you'd act as a sight-seeing guide on this trip, Prentiss.   Being an Englishman, you ought to know this country like the back of your hand.   How about pointing out the sights?"

"That's a swell idea, Bob," cut in Don.   "Come on, Eric, let's hear your spiel."

"Righto," laughed Eric.   "Here goes.   Now on your right, gentlemen, you have the great city of London, largest city in the world and the capital of the British Empire.   That thin, winding strip of water over which we are now passing is the famous Thames River.   It doesn't look like much from this end, but you should see it on the other side of London.

"If you'll take a glance over your starboard wing," went on Eric, "you'll see the towers of Windsor

Castle, and in the distance is Oxford University. And after that, we'll be passing over the Shakespeare country—Stratford-on-Avon, Warwick. . . ."

"And after that," cut in a strange voice, "you may run into a bunch of Stuka dive bombers, so you'd better keep your eyes peeled and cut out this Cook's Tour. You may be revealing information to the enemy."

From then on, Don and Bob had to be content with watching the scenery in si   ce. It had not oc-curred to them that enemy airc   might be active on such a clear day, although t   all knew that Stuka dive bombers—particularly   new JU 88— were carrying out daring daylight r   's. Usually, however, they chose days with low-   ng clouds, where they could quickly conceal thems   ves when necessary.

Eric led them in a wide detour around the indus-trial section of Birmingham, continuing to bear northeast. Their ground speed was increased by a following wind from the south. It seemed to Bob that they had been in the air only twenty minutes when Eric shot the nose of his Spitfire down and dived toward the ground. Bob and Don went screaming after him. Then Eric pulled around into a tight right-hand bank and again the boys followed his lead. Now their starboard wings were pointed at a magnificent cathedral.

"In order to avoid giving information to the enemy," said Eric, "I can only say that a Civil War president of the United States bore the same name as this cathedral."

Straightening out, Eric now led them due north, above a completely different kind of countryside. There was very little sign of industry, and to the east the landscape was as flat as a board. To the west, the horizon was blotted out by heavy smoke.

"Behind that smoke," Eric started his geography game again, "is a field. And who do you suppose would be cooking out in the middle of a field, or do either of you birds happen to know any French?"

"Of course," thought Bob, "that would be Sheffield."

"Soon," continued Eric, "we'll be by-passing a large city, the name of which I cannot give you, but if a ship didn't have one, it wouldn't float."

Making a wide circuit to the right of Hull, the planes passed out over the North Sea and the entrance to Hull Harbor on the Humber River. Then Eric led them back to land and for perhaps fifty miles they passed over the wild Yorkshire Moors.

"Soon," began Eric again, "we'll be coming to the kind of place where kings live. That is," he added, "the few kings that are left. Only this is the more modern version. You'll recognize it by the heavy smoke screen. In other words, you won't be able to see anything."

Bob gathered at once that Eric was referring to Newcastle-on-Tyne. Ever mindful of the serious side of their present trip, Bob kept a watchful eye for the enemy.

"Cut it, Eric," he called urgently a few moments later. "If I'm not mistaken, those are enemy aircraft coming in over the coast."

"I think you're right, Bob," replied Eric. "Let's have a look-see."

The aircraft had approached under cover of a haze over the water, and Bob had just managed to glimpse them at a moment when the sun flashed on their wings. Headed for the pall of smoke that lay ahead, they were flying several thousand feet below the Spitfires.

Swiftly Eric maneuvered his flight into the sun before beginning the dive. They were enemy aircraft all right, and the black crosses on their wings were clearly visible. Not only that, they were JU 88's—the new twin-engined Stuka dive bombers.

The Jerries were now approaching a small town along the coast where a number of cargo ships were tied up at the large docks. These ships were unquestionably the Stukas' target.

The Jerries now peeled off and dived for the piers with a head start of several thousand feet. Could the Spitfires overtake them? Or would the Stukas release their deadly bombs before Bob and Don and Eric were able to close within range?

Quickly Eric ordered a change in formation. "O.K., fellows, one, two, three, and remember the cannon."

Bob knew what that meant. Eric would take the first diving ship, he the second, and Don the third. In spite of the two grim muzzles sticking out from his wings, Bob had forgotten about the cannon. Now, he realized, he would be able to open fire at a much greater distance than if he had only machine guns.

As they dived, Bob saw the needle on the air-speed indicator pass the five hundred mile an hour mark. How much farther it went, he never knew. Boosting his engine, he tore after Eric like a meteor. Somewhere behind him was Don. It would be a ticklish matter to ... ... his guns to bear on the second Stuka and at the same time avoid striking Eric's plane. But Eric had simplified the situation by swinging wide for a deflection.

Their speed was now more than twice that of the diving Stukas. If only they could close in before the Jerries released their bombs. Paralleling Eric's line of flight, Bob plunged on. At any moment now the Stukas would release their missiles of death. Close enough to take in every grim detail of his quarry's lines, Bob saw the air flaps extend to slow down the diving speed. There was no sign of enemy pilots or crew, however. Then Bob remembered that no heads would be visible as the crew would be lying down, guiding their craft and its bombs by a system of optical reflection sights. The attack was apparently quite unexpected, as there was no anti-aircraft fire from the ground. Or perhaps the

ground defenders had seen the attacking Spitfires
and were holding their fire.

One of the Stukas was now full in his sights and
Bob squeezed the button, releasing the full power of
his six machine guns and two cannon. The results
were unexpected and very nearly disastrous—to Bob.
The terrific bucking of the cannon fire threw him
slightly off his line and his shells flew through the
Jerry's afterfuselage instead of through the forward
part as he had planned. The Stuka pilot, caught
completely unawares, tried desperately to pull away
from the fire of the Spitter.

"At least," thought Bob, "I've ruined his aim."
So great was Bob's speed compared to his adversary's
that he had no time for a second burst and, pulling
around, almost crashed into the following Stuka.
He only hoped that Don would hold his fire until
he got around. Bob's quarry now streaked for the
shelter of the smoke pall ahead and his speed began
to pick up. Bob poured everything he could into
the Merlin and saw the air-speed indicator quiver
around four hundred miles an hour.

Down below, one of the other Stukas plummeted

toward the earth, a mass of flames. That must have been Eric's work. Now if only Don had been lucky, too. Closing in on the fleeing Stuka, Bob watched the Jerry race desperately for the enveloping smoke. Bob was sure that he could get him, but as he came within possible range, the Stuka banked to the right and again dived toward the target. This time the wing flaps were up and his speed was much greater. Banking over, Bob plunged after him. This time there must be no mistake.

Again with his superior speed he closed within range. As he did so, he noted that around the Stuka from wing tip to nose and from wing tip to tail there was a huge ring, evidently designed to ward off balloon barrage cables. Prepared, this time, for the terrific bucking from the cannon fire, Bob coolly squeezed the button. His burst entered the fuselage on the starboard side of the Stuka just above the wing. The results were instant and terrible. The whole aircraft seemed to disintegrate in the air, and Bob could see bits of the Stuka as they were flung out in a sheet of flame ahead. The concussion almost turned him over, and he knew then that his burst must have detonated the bombs carried by the Jerry.

The Stuka's pilot and air crew had no chance, for there was nothing left of the aircraft. It had simply burst into pieces. Instinctively Bob had pulled wide, and as he banked dizzily around, a section of the Stuka's wing came fluttering down from 〈...〉ve. Eagerly he scanned the skies for Don or Eric, b〈...〉 they were nowhere in sight. Then off in the smoke he saw a reddish glow screaming earthward. That would be Don's Stuka, or might it be Don himself?

"O.K., fellows," came Eric's cheery voice over the R.T. "Nice work. Let's re-form at a thousand over the piers."

Shoving hard over, Bob banked steeply for the rendezvous. This almost instant response probably saved his life. As his wing came up, he felt a rasping grind and he dropped steeply, his left wing tip pointing toward the earth. The Spitfire dropped into a spin, but recovering quickly, Bob shot the nose up towards the sky. Then he saw what had happened, and he went cold with sudden fright. Dotting the sky all around him were balloons. They had flown into the middle of a balloon barrage, and one of the cables had caught Bob's wing.

"Eric! Eric!" Bob shouted into the R.T. "We're right in the middle of a balloon barrage."

Pointing the nose up, Bob spiraled steeply. Thank heaven for the power in the faithful Merlin that made it possible for him to stand almost on his tail. Up and up he climbed until he reached twenty-five thousand feet. Sucking oxygen, he cruised a bit, looking down on the balloon tops with the cloud crests beneath. He flew well out to sea before he dared come down, and then he dove steeply to three thousand feet. Coming into the coast, the town materialized in the sea haze, and there he saw Don and Eric cruising back and forth waiting for him.

"Was that a close one!" called Bob over the R.T. "One of the cables just grazed my wing tip but, so far as I can see, no damage has been done."

"We certainly were lucky," said Eric. "If anything had happened, you'd have had me to thank for it. Stupidly enough, I didn't see those balloons. As a matter of fact, I think they were hidden completely when we came over. But I should have had enough sense to know that even a small port like this would be protected."

"Oh, forget it, Eric," said Don. "It's all Bob's

fault anyway; he was the one who got us into this mess. If he hadn't been so nosy, he wouldn't have seen those Stukas."

"Just the same," said Eric, "I'm sure glad he did see them, for it means three Stukas less for the Luftwaffe and probably three more cargo ships for us. If those babies had released their bombs, there isn't much doubt about the result. But let's get going. The first thing we know, we'll be late getting to Edinburgh."

"Nice work, Spitters," came in a voice over the headphone. "Those Jerries sort of crossed us up. We're glad you were in the vicinity. Your victories will be confirmed."

"You're very welcome," replied Prentiss. "Don't forget the confirmations. We'll be coming in to see you again sometime."

"Hold on tight, you fellows," called out Eric over the R.T., "we've got some smoke to go through, but we ought to be in the clear in about ten minutes, and in another twenty we should be in Edinburgh."

"What, no more quiz programs, Eric?" called out Don.

"I think that's about enough quiz for one day,"

replied Eric, laughing into his mike, "but we'll see."

Through smoke-laden skies the Spitfires roared on above the mining and industrial districts of Northumberland to emerge in the clear some ten minutes later. Dropping down to their assigned flight level, they cruised above a sparsely settled countryside. To the right, the North Sea was pounding against a rocky coast line, and here and there was a wide stretch of sandy beach.

They were now approaching Holy Island which lies directly off the Northeasternmost coast of England.

"It may interest you boys to know," said Eric, "that that island off the coast is not an island at low tide. In fact, I've walked there many times from the shore. Sorry I can't give you the name, but at the risk of having Intelligence go crazy trying to decode our messages, I'll tell you this much. When your toe goes through the end of your sock, what do you have?"

"A sore toe, of course," answered Don.

"That's right," agreed Eric, "but what does your sock have?"

"Oh, I get it," said Bob, "and you'll wear a hole in

your sock climbing the lee side of the island. Is that right?"

"Bright boy," replied Eric. "It's certainly nice," he added, "to feel that you're flying in the company of such smart pilots."

Bob was fascinated with the beauty of the wild countryside beneath. But while it was wild and desolate, there was ample evidence along the coast that any attempts at invasion would not come as a surprise.

"Now," said Eric as they flashed over a river, "I hope it's not revealing a military secret to say that we've left England and are flying over bonnie Scotland. For the next fifteen minutes, there will be no quiz programs, so keep your eyes on your rear-vision mirrors and let me know if there's any excitement."

Leaving the coast line, Eric led his flight east of north. A few minutes later a wide expanse of water appeared directly ahead. Cutting even further east, they soon came within view of a large city.

This was Edinburgh, and Bob thought it the most beautiful sight he had ever seen from the air. He hoped that he would have a chance to explore it from the ground. Even from five thousand feet he could make out the beautiful Princess Street Gardens and the great Castle Rock. In less than a minute they had cleared the city limits and directly ahead was the great bridge across the Firth of Forth —a frequent target for Nazi bombers.

Eric carefully avoided that vicinity and swung south. In a few moments, with engines cut, they were settling down on the runway at their destination. With a squealing of brakes, the three boys stopped their Spitfires on the tarmac and stiffly clambered out of their narrow cockpits.

CHAPTER V

Secret Bomber Base

"What delayed you fellows?" asked the Briefing Officer as soon as they checked in at the Operations Office. "You had us a bit worried."

"We were slightly delayed south of Newcastle, sir," replied Eric, "but it couldn't be helped." He went on to tell of the Nazi dive-bombing attack on the ships at the small coast port.

"Better late than never, I suppose," said the Briefing Officer. "Hurry up now and make out your report. The C.O. is waiting to talk to you."

"Yes, sir," the pilots replied in unison, and immediately sat down at a long table to record their flight and explain their unexpected detour. A few minutes later they were in the C.O.'s office.

"I'm glad you chaps brought those Spitters in safely," began the Commanding Officer. "We need them badly. According to these reports," he glanced again at the papers on his desk, "you gave them a little workout on the way up."

"That's right, sir," responded Eric. "Sorry we were a little late getting in."

"I wish you chaps could stay with us," went on the C.O. "We could use you. But I have orders from London to send you over to the Bomber Command as quickly as possible, that is, to headquarters in Edinburgh. I'll arrange for a car to take you over to the city. In the meantime, why don't you cut on over to the dispersal hut. I think you'll find some coffee and sandwiches there."

"A fine idea, sir," declared the always hungry Don.

As they entered the dispersal hut, the loud-speaker began calling out, "Red Squadron, scramble. Red Squadron, scramble."

The pilots abruptly left their coffee and sandwiches and dashed for the door, almost knocking down the three who were entering.

"This is certainly a break for us," said Don. "If those men had stuck around there might not have been any food left."

"Help yourselves," said one of the remaining pilots, pushing over a plate piled high with sandwiches. "Here, orderly," he called, "three more cups of Java. My name's Benson," he said, noting the U.S.A. on Terrell's shoulder, "and I'm from Oklahoma. Where are you from?"

"Terrell, from Texas," replied Bob. "This is Pilot Officer White and Flying Officer Prentiss."

"Glad to know you chaps," Benson declared. "Hope you'll be sticking around for awhile."

"I wish we were," Bob said, "but they're sending us over to the Bomber Command right away."

"You too, eh?" replied Benson. "They've been transferring quite a number of chaps, and that's why we're so short of fighter pilots around here. Would you mind if I ride over to Edinburgh with you? I have to report to headquarters, too. If there's time, maybe I can show you a bit of the town."

"Splendid," replied Eric. "We could use a guide. I'm just as much of a foreigner up here in Scotland as Bob and Don."

A short time later the four boys were on the ferry crossing the Firth of Forth to Edinburgh.

"You fellows may think," explained Benson, "that you have all the excitement down there on the south coast, but, believe me, we have plenty of it up here. You can understand why," he added, pointing to the heavily loaded ships passing up and down the harbor. "Jerry has been trying out daylight attacks with his new twin-engined Stukas."

"Yes, we found that out," smiled Bob, telling of their experience on the co south of Newcastle.

"Great Scott!" exclaimed Benson. "You fellows really did a good job. Those babies are tough and they're fast. You were lucky to come at them in their dive."

Leaving the dock, their car passed through the narrow streets near the waterfront up to the wider avenues of New Edinburgh.

"That's the Sir Walter Scott Monument," said Benson, pointing to a high structure in the park that faced the beautiful Princess Street. "But you can't see much of it because of the sandbags."

"Do you get much bombing up here?" asked Don.

"Yes, plenty," answered Benson, "but most of it before I arrived on the scene. As a matter of fact, the first big Jerry raid on the British Isles was an attack on Edinburgh."

Leaving Benson a few minutes later, the three pilots presented themselves before the Air Officer Commanding, who told them that a car would be waiting at two o'clock to take them to an airdrome north of Edinburgh. From that point they would be flown to their destination.

"What about our luggage, sir?" asked Eric. "It should be at the station now. Where will we have it shipped, sir?"

"That's already been taken care of," said the A.O.C. smiling. "Sorry I can't tell you where you're headed. You may think there's a lot of mystery about this business, but you'll understand better when you arrive."

"Mystery is right," said Eric when they had left the A.O.C.'s office. "I'm beginning to think we've landed in a mystery novel by mistake."

There was no sign of Benson, who had agreed to meet them at the door, so the three boys waited. After fifteen minutes Bob suggested, "Perhaps we'd better inquire for him; maybe he had to leave in a hurry."

Just then Benson came toward them, beaming. "What do you know, fellows? I'm going along with you—wherever that is. They wouldn't give me any information at all, except that I am to leave at two o'clock in a car for an airdrome up north, and they're forwarding my stuff directly from the squadron."

"That's grand," said Bob, delighted that the American was going to be with them. "It will give us time to see something of the city before we leave."

"Let's find a good restaurant and celebrate," suggested Don.

"Oh, oh," said Eric, "there he goes again." He went on to explain to Benson about Don's affinity for food.

"I'll tell you what," said their new companion, "I'm rather hungry myself, but I think we'll have time to go up to the castle before we leave. That's something you ought to see. We may be so isolated at the Bomber Squadron that there might not be another chance."

To save time the boys took a taxi, and in a few minutes they had climbed to the top of the Great Rock. The castle perched above it seemed to be growing right out of the rock itself.

"I wanted you to see this," explained Benson, "because it helps you to understand what kind of fighters these Scotsmen are."

The four boys walked slowly through the great

War Memorial, filled with the flags and the crests of the great Scottish regiments and the names of those who had fallen in World War I.

"These Scots are certainly some fighters," remarked Don.

"You can double that," said Roy Benson, "as you'll be finding out that they make fine pilots. Some of the best pilots in our squadron are Scots."

On the way down from the castle their new friend pointed out some of the other interesting sights of Edinburgh.

"There's John Knox's home," he said, indicating a building in one of the narrow streets, "and that's the famous St. Giles Cathedral."

"How about pointing out a good restaurant now," suggested Don.

"O.K.," laughed Benson. "I can see that history means nothing to you when your stomach is calling."

During the meal, at the largest restaurant the boys could find, they speculated on the new type of bombers they soon would be flying. Benson said there had been a lot of talk about them at his squadron. He was so interested that he had talked to the

C.O. about being transferred and had expressed his willingness to be shifted to the new bomber squadron. Nothing further had been said about it, however, and today's orders had come as a complete surprise to him.

"All we really know," said Eric, "is that these new bombers are fast and very maneuverable. But how they can carry an adequate load of bombs is something that I can't figure out."

"Looks like we'll just have to wait to find out," said Bob. "And at the rate they're pushing us through, it won't be long."

As they crossed the great bridge over the Firth of Forth on their way back to headquarters Benson called their attention to the large cargo vessels headed in each direction.

"That gives you some idea why the Stuka bombers are busy around here," he explained.

In less than ten minutes after they reached the airdrome, the four pilots were airborne in an Avro-Anson.

"We have about an hour's trip ahead of us," announced their pilot, a Royal Air Force Lieutenant,

through innumerable gullies. After rounding a hill, Bob could see smooth green runways which blended perfectly with the turf.

"That's the airdrome," said the Flight Lieutenant, "and here are the hangars," he added, taxiing around another hill.

Recesses had been cut right into the foot of a hill and not until they had actually reached the entrance was there any evidence of a base. Taxiing beneath an overhanging apron that seemed to be part of the hill itself, the Flight Lieutenant cut the engine and the boys piled out. They had reached the secret bomber base at last.

The great natural hangar was a beehive of activity. Great reinforced concrete pillars supported the rock ceiling but left ample space for the maneuvering and storing of planes. The Flight Lieutenant led the four pilots across to an office on one side.

"Four more new pilots, sir," he said, saluting a Wing Commander.

"Thank you, Smithfield," replied the Wing Commander. "I was afraid you might run into some trouble on the way up. The Jerries have just been unloading a few more tons on our decoy."

"We saw them, but I'm quite sure they didn't see us, thanks to Flying Off r Terrell who managed to spot them way do e line."

Smithfield the o duced the four pilots to Wing Commander ar urne.

"Gentle n, re glad to have you here. We're pretty ten track but I hope you'll find it in esti g You're probably curious about what w e d ng p here and I'll try to explain some of the ystery.

First of all, we have a new type of bomber about which Jerry would give his eyeteeth to have further information. Although none of them has been flown out of the country, somehow, someway, Jerry has found out about it. Not the details, we hope, but merely the fact that we're about ready to spring a surprise on him. If you can contain your patience until after dinner, I'll try to tell you the whole story. In the meantime, Smithfield, let them have a look."

CHAPTER VI

ENTER THE STRATOHAWKS

"THERE they are, fellows," said the Flight Lieutenant proudly. "We've nicknamed them Stratohawks."

"Gosh!" said Don, drawing in his breath sharply and completely forgetting about food. "This job looks like a cross between a Martin Maryland and a Lockheed Lightning."

"That's just about the size of it," agreed Smithfield. "They have the speed of Lightnings and the sting of Marylands."

Fascinated, the four pilots could not take their eyes from this wicked-looking, twin-engined aircraft.

"How long before we'll have a chance to fly one of these?" asked Bob eagerly.

"I'm sure I don't know, Terrell," replied Smithfield, "but probably within a few days. You fellows are the last to arrive of the pilots chosen to do this work, and the C.O. probably will give you all the dope tonight."

The four fliers reported to the Adjutant in one of the low buildings at some distance from the camouflaged hillside hangar.

"How would you fellows like to bunk?" questioned the Adjutant.

"I'm not really with these chaps," said Benson quickly.

"Oh, yes you are now," cut in Eric. "Could you put us all together, sir?"

"I think that can be arranged," replied the Adjutant. "You may have to get along without your gear until morning, unless it comes in on a night train. If so, it will be picked up and delivered to you at the hut."

"Oh, we'll manage, sir," replied Eric.

"I think we'd better separate these two Yanks," suggested Don. "Otherwise, they'll keep us awake talking all night. How about bunking with me, Benson?"

"That's O.K. with me," replied Benson, pleased at being accepted so quickly as a friend by his new acquaintances.

"Well, I guess that means I'll have to put up with you, Bob," said Eric.

"I wonder," said Don plaintively, "when dinner will be served."

"Say, this fellow doesn't eat all night, does he?" inquired Benson in an alarmed voice.

"Not quite," answered Bob, "but it's a good idea to keep some chocolate bars around to quiet him."

Having no luggage to unpack, the boys decided to inspect the station while waiting for dinner.

"Do you realize, fellows," said Eric suddenly, "that we must be at least five hundred miles north of London right now?"

"At least that," agreed Benson. "Which means that the nearest Nazi bases are in Norway. At least that's where most of our attacks on Edinburgh are supposed to have originated."

"I've always wanted to see a bomber operations room," said Bob. "Let's go over to the officers' mess and inquire where it is."

At the mess the boys found about twenty other pilots who had been transferred from various fighter squadrons throughout the country, and they, too, were anxiously awaiting information about the new bombers. Bob was especially happy to meet several fellow Americans.

Upon inquiring for the operations room, the boys were told that they probably would not be very welcome and that they had better wait for the Wing Commander's talk which would come immediately after dinner. This was entirely different from a fighter station, and for the first time Bob began to feel a little sorry that he had left Y Squadron.

Practically all the conversation in the mess centered about the new bombers and a dive-bombing attack by the Jerries that afternoon. Bob learned that the point bombed was several miles away from the squadron quarters. So far, the Jerries had failed to find the actual base and every precaution was being taken that they should not find it.

The excited speculation preceding dinner gave way to a strained silence during the meal. Eric was seated beside Bob, and Don and Roy Benson were on the other side. They all were waiting eagerly to hear from the Commanding Officer.

While the coffee was being served, Wing Commander Cranbourne rose from his seat and announced, "As soon as you've finished, gentlemen, come into the lounge and we'll get started."

On this particular occasion there was none of the usual lingering over coffee. Almost as if in response to a military command, cups were lifted and drained and chairs were pushed back from the table.

"You chaps," began the Commanding Officer when they had gathered in the lounge, "seem almost as anxious to hear what I have to say as I am to say it. First of all, it's only fair to tell you that you're in for a period of mighty hard work. I'm going to have to crowd you awfully hard.

"As fighter pilots, you will have a lot to learn before we can get started, but I'm anxious to cut down the instruction period as much as possible. What we are planning is in the nature of a huge experiment which will help to determine our future bombing strategy against the enemy.

"All of you have seen the new plane and I can tell you, having flown it, that it's a marvel. Until you are ready for action, your time will be divided between flying and ground study. There will be little free time and no leaves whatsoever. The finest air observers in the R.A.F. have been chosen to act as your navigators. The first training flights will begin at eight o'clock tomorrow morning. Now are there any questions?" He paused and glanced quickly over the eager faces before him.

"What range do the Stratohawks have, sir?" inquired a pilot sitting near Bob.

"Approximately three thousand miles with a full bomb load," was the reply.

This answer provoked an excited burst of conversation among the pilots.

"I should add," continued the Wing Commander, "that the name 'Stratohawk' is not official, but it wo_ _do any harm if the enemy hears it. You'll understa__ _ _r what I mean when we go into action. Any further qu_ _ons with regard to its characteristics can wait unti_ _ _'ve flown the aircraft. But just to relieve your curiosity a little, I can tell you now that it will fly faster than anything you've flown, and we believe its ceiling is high enough to overfly anything the enemy has to offer. Now we'll run off a motion picture of an air raid on a hostile target. The aircraft in the picture are Wellingtons, but the general procedure is much the same as that which you will follow. Notice particularly the coordination among air crew members. As fighter pilots who have been on your own, you may have to give special thought to this phase."

As soon as the Wing Commander finished speaking, the lights were dimmed and the film was thrown on the screen. Bob thought it was the most thrilling picture he had ever seen. The movie showed everything from the briefing of the bomber's crew on the take-off to the bombing of the enemy objective and the perilous return over the North Sea to the home base. When it was finished, every pilot in the room felt that he had learned more about the Bomber Command in those few minutes than he could from an hour's lecture.

"It looks as if we're in for something a lot bigger than we've guessed," remarked Eric soberly.

"I think so, too," agreed Bob.

The days that followed were busy ones for every pilot in the squadron, for there was much to learn in a very short time. Instead of further training on the Avro-Ansons, the Commander started them right off on the Stratohawk, explaining that he did not want them to get too heavy-handed on the controls.

The first time Bob climbed through the low belly hatch of the Stratohawk he knew that this flight would be the highlight of his flying experiences to date. And he was not disappointed.

"O.K., Terrell. Come on up here and squeeze in beside me," said Wing Commander Cranbourne.

"Yes, sir," said Bob. "Squeeze" was certainly the right word. The cabin was small and compact, most of the space being given over to the bomb well. The slick streamlining of the upper fuselage left scant room for two pilots side by side.

"That's the only disadvantage I can find about this baby," elaborated the Wing Commander. "It's a pretty tight fit for the pilots. You may have noticed, Terrell, that all the lads we picked for this job are pretty slim."

This was the first time that Bob had received flight instruction from a Wing Commander. As soon as his seat belt was fastened, Wing Commander Cranbourne released the brakes and, gunning the engines slightly, taxied down through the gullies toward the central field.

"Just the two of us, sir?" asked Bob in a tone of real surprise.

"Yes, just the two of us. We won't need a navigator on this trip. The ordinary complement is two pilots and one air observer as navigator. The second pilot, or copilot, will double as the wireless operator.

"You'll notice, Terrell, that there's only one runway here—up and down the valley. Whatever the wind direction, there's always a strong draft one way or the other along the valley. This morning it's from the south, so we'll take off to the south. There are no windsocks here to identify the place, so I'll show you how to check on your landing directions." Then, to Bob's complete amazement, "I want you to take her off."

"Take her off, sir?" Bob was startled.

"Why, certainly," said the Wing Commander. "Smithfield told me you had the controls in the Anson coming up, so you know how to handle the throttles. Simply take her off as you would a Spitfire."

Bob tried hard to imagine himself back in the familiar Spitfire cockpit. He was tempted to shove the throttles forward and let her go, but instead, he checked the brakes and tested his engine. Then, glancing quickly at the instruments, he released the brakes and firmly gunned the engines. He had never before felt such a surge of power, and almost instantly the wheels left the ground. The Wing Commander reached forward and pushed the under-carriage retraction button.

The Stratohawk seemed to leap upward with hardly any pull on the stick. Bob noticed that he was ruddering hard to the right, so he eased off slightly on the starboard engine throttle. This was the most incredible airplane that Bob had ever flown. No wonder everyone had been so secretive about it. He could only guess at how much power might be stored in those engines. Unbelievingly, he watched the air-speed indicator and the tachometers which registered the engine revolutions. At the cruising mark the speed was above three hundred miles an hour and less than two minutes after the take-off the altimeter was registering four thousand feet. And he had not really tried to climb her yet!

"O.K., Terrell, that's fine," praised the Wing Commander. "I'll take over for a bit now. No doubt you're wondering just what she really will do," he added, smiling.

"I certainly am, sir," replied the delighted Bob. "I've never seen anything like it."

As the Wing Commander poured in the power, he pulled back gently on the stick. The Stratohawk climbed almost straight up, not for just a second, but on and on without any sign of falling off from the climb. At fifteen thousand feet the Wing Commander motioned to Bob to fasten his oxygen tube. He dropped the nose slightly, but still they climbed —twenty, twenty-five, and finally thirty thousand feet. They were now flying several thousand feet above the topmost of the cloud tips. During this rapid climb Cranbourne had been manipulating certain controls on the dash that were unfamiliar to Bob.

"Now," said the Wing Commander, "I want to show you something. We haven't much time or I'd take you higher, but you'll have plenty of opportunity to do that on your own."

In the thin, rarefied air of the substratosphere the Wing Commander put the Stratohawk through a series of maneuvers that left Bob actually breathless.

"Well, Terrell," he finally asked, "what do you think of her?"

"I think she's marvelous, sir," gasped Bob.

"Do you notice anything in particular?"

"Do you mean aside from the maneuverability, sir?"

"Yes. Aside from that."

"It seems to be much more comfortable at this height in the Stratohawk than it is in a Spitfire," answered Bob.

"Do you know why?"

"I think I do," said Bob. "This is a pressure-sealed cabin, isn't it?"

"That's right. You're actually sitting in a pressure equivalent to only eight thousand feet." He then showed Bob how to manipulate the dials for the supercharging of the cabin.

"It's a very simple principle," explained the Wing Commander, "but it's taken a lot of painstaking research. Just as the engines have to be supercharged for efficiency in the rare air of the higher altitudes, so does the body require it. Suppose you take over now and we'll go down."

Bob wanted to stay up longer, but instead he eased off on the throttle, descending in wide, lazy spirals through the cumulus clouds. Noting the cluster of buildings that the Nazis had bombed, he tried his best to find the narrow strip from which they had taken off, but it was too well camouflaged, and the Wing Commander had to point out the identifying marks to him.

"Not bad, Terrell. That's the closest anyone has come to it yet," praised Cranbourne. "Now notice your drift. These hills run due east and west. If your drift is to the north, then you land to the south. If it's to the south, you land to the north. We've checked it very carefully, and there are no cross winds in the valley. O.K., take her down."

Bob lowered his undercarriage, dropped the wing flaps, eased back on his throttle, and slid down the valley to the runway.

"Gun her slightly, Terrell," advised the Wing Commander.

Bob flew the Stratohawk in without the Wing Commander's touching the controls. This was the kind of instruction he liked.

"Good work, Terrell," said the Wing Commander as he taxied in. "I think you'll be all right from now on. Not much different from flying a fighter, is it?"

"Not much," agreed Bob, "except that it feels as if you were hanging on to two Spitfires instead of one."

"That's about the size of it," laughed the Wing Commander.

"There's one thing I don't understand, sir," said Bob. "I had expected to use even more throttle for the landing."

"No, Terrell. That's one of the finest features about this plane. All we need to know, however, is that they do the job, and the enemy must never learn how it is done. In order to protect this secret, there's a little switch here beneath this glass. One minute after the glass is broken and the switch is turned, a delayed action fuse will detonate explosives in the petrol tanks which will destroy the aircraft. Remember, Terrell, we cannot let any of these new planes fall into the hands of the enemy."

Several pilots were waiting for their turn in the Stratohawk when Bob and the Wing Commander taxied up to the hangar. Among them were Eric, Don, and Roy Benson, none of whom had yet flown the new ship. They advanced on Bob excitedly as he descended from the plane.

"What's it like, Bob?" they chorused.

"It's like two Spitfires harnessed together," said Bob.

"Send Mr. Prentiss in," called out Wing Commander Cranbourne.

"You'll get a great thrill, Eric," predicted Bob as Eric crawled up through the hole in the floor of the fuselage.

The class work was intensive and difficult, but so keen was the interest of the pilots that no one seemed to mind the pressure. There was so much to learn—the intimate details of the aircraft itself and also the procedure on bombing raids. They must learn not only their own work, but the method of cooperation between pilot and navigator. The copilot, in addition to acting as relief pilot, had to take over the ordinary functions of the wireless air gunner. The air observer, or navigator, plotted the course and directed the pilot and acted as the bombardier when the target was reached.

The different kinds of bombs and the purposes of each—the heavy demolition type, fragmentation bomb, and the incendiaries—formed a separate phase of their study. The type of bomb to be used depended on the bombing mission and the height from which the bombs were to be dropped. Weather, the greatest ally or hazard in long-range bombing raids, was thoroughly studied in meteorology classes. The Stratohawk, with its high ceiling, could climb well above any icy condition and other inclement weather.

Then there was intensive study of the enemy anti-aircraft positions and searchlight corridors so that the pilots and navigators could plot the safest courses and determine the best means of approaching the target.

After dinner the boys usually held a bunk flying session in Bob's room. Each of them had now flown the Stratohawk with Wing Commander Cranbourne and each was loud in his praise of the plane's performance.

"By the way, Bob," said Eric one evening, "the C.O. paid you quite a high compliment when I was flying with him."

"What was it?"

"He said you caught on fast and were just the kind of pilot they wanted for this work."

"I'm certainly glad to hear it. How did you get along, Eric?"

"Not bad, once I got off the ground, but he did make me do a second landing."

"Second landing!" exclaimed Don. "I had to do four. He bawled the living daylights out of me. He asked me what was wrong with me and was I nervous. And I said no, I was just hungry."

"By the way, Don," spoke up Roy Benson, "I found out today what food we'll be carrying along with us on these long-range bombing flights. As far as I can gather, the average rations consist of a few biscuits, an apple or an orange, a bar of chocolate, barley sugar, chewing gum, and raisins."

"That doesn't sound like much," said Don sadly.

"Wait a minute, that isn't all," added Roy. "You also get some hot coffee or tea in a vacuum flask."

"Maybe," said Don hopefully, "I'll draw a navigator who becomes air sick and won't be able to eat his rations. That would help."

"The thing that puzzles me," said Bob, "is how they can hope to keep these planes secret when the Jerries are raiding us as far north as this."

"As I understand it," replied Eric, "there are patrols in the air all the time we're flying and ground spotters are on the alert. If any enemy aircraft are sighted or picked up, there is plenty of warning to hide the Stratohawks."

"All I hope," went on Bob, "is that I can be up in the air when something comes along. I'm looking forward to handling one of these babies in a dogfight."

"I don't imagine," said Roy Benson, "that any of us will have to wait very long for that."

CHAPTER VII

A Coincidence?

The following week was filled with intensive ground and flight training. Bob was now completely at home in the new aircraft. He, Eric, and Roy Benson had moved up as captains of their planes, but Don was held back as second pilot.

"I don't think Cranbourne likes me," said Don as the four boys walked back to their quarters from the hangar.

"That isn't it at all, Don. Wing Commander Cranbourne was telling me what a fine wireless operator you are. He found out about your 'ham' experience back home. When he mentioned it to me, I told him it would be great if you and I could be flying together."

"Wait a minute, there," said Roy Benson. "I'd like to have Don flying with me."

"Where do I come in?" asked Eric.

"Now wait a minute, you fellows," said Don, whose disappointment was somewhat lessened by his friends' desire for his services, "I'll tell you what I'll do. I'm hard to get, but I'll sell out to the man offering me the best food, and I don't mean just quality, I mean quantity."

When the air crew lists were posted that evening, Bob was pleased to find Don assigned to his plane. He did not know the Sergeant Air Observer who was posted as his navigator.

The entire group was called together in the lounge after dinner, and Wing Commander Cranbourne talked to them informally.

"You have done a fine job these last two weeks," he began, "and I want to thank you for your cooperation. It hasn't been easy on any of us, but I'm hoping the results will warrant the effort we've put forth.

"You may have noticed that the air crews are now posted on the bulletin board. Some of you may be surprised that you have been made captains of your aircraft and others may be disappointed to find that you are still second pilots. I've done my best in making these assignments and have tried to take into consideration your individual qualifications and abilities. Tomorrow morning at eight you are to report to the Briefing Room where you will meet your assigned air observers. Following that, we will have cross-country maneuvers, each aircraft being manned by the allotted crew."

"I wonder what kind of navigator we've drawn," said Bob, as the pilots resumed their seats after the Wing Commander had left. "I only hope he knows his way about."

"So do I," agreed Don. "Even a delicate chap with a finicky stomach might be able to do that."

"Listen," said Bob, "just remember that I don't want our cabin cluttered up with crumbs."

"Meaning who, sir?" asked Don meekly. "You or me or the navigator?"

"I mean your blessed food, you lug," said Bob disgustedly.

Fortunately, they didn't have long to wonder about their new navigator.

"Flying Officer Terrell, sir?" inquired a short, stocky Sergeant Air Observer early the following morning.

"Why, yes, Sergeant," replied Bob. "That's my name."

"Well, sir," responded the Sergeant, "I believe I'm

to be your navigator. My name's McTavish, sir, sometimes called Sandy."

Noting the thick thatch of red hair sticking out beneath his cap, Bob could readily understand the source of the nickname. He also noticed the ribbons beneath the single wing on McTavish's chest.

McTavish, in turn, was making his own appraisal.

"I see you've done a bit of flying yourself, sir." His gaze dropped to the diagonally striped ribbon beneath Bob's double wings.

"Well, a little," admitted Bob, "but I must confess that I don't know much about bombers."

"There's little to it, sir, and you'll find it comes very easy," McTavish answered reassuringly. "As for myself, I've found a most monotonous life. Long hours and the lack of food are very wearing on a man. It isn't the quality of the food, mind you, it's the quantity."

"This is Sergeant McTavish, Don," said Bob, turning to his companion. "Pilot Officer Don White," he finished the introduction. "Mr. White will be flying with us, Sergeant."

"Glad to know you, sir," said McTavish, extending a gnarled hand. "I was just telling Mr. Terrell," went on the Sergeant, "that I've found this bombing to be a most monotonous life. The hours are long and the food insufficient."

"The food?" repeated Don weakly.

"Aye," said McTavish. " 'Tis a great pity. A man needs plenty of nourishment for this work. But I'm sure," he added unsmilingly, "that we'll get along very fine together."

"I'm sure we will, too," agreed Bob. "Come on," he said to the unhappy looking Don, "let's get down to the hangar. You look as if you'd lost your last friend."

"I knew something like this would happen to me," Don wailed.

"I beg your pardon, sir?" asked McTavish.

"Oh, nothing, Sergeant," said Don. "I was just thinking."

"It's a bad habit so soon after breakfast," said Mc-Tavish. "Ye mustna let it interfere with your digestion."

Don was still looking pretty glum as they took off.

"Come now," said Bob, "it isn't as bad as that.

I'm the one that should be unhappy, for you'll both be trying to get my rations. Take over for awhile, will you, Don?"

The various air crews had been assigned to specific cross-country runs, each ship carrying practice bombs equivalent to the normal bombing load.

"Hello, sir," said McTavish, "your course is XX."

Don banked tightly to port and was soon on course. It was a cloudy day and the ground was visible only now and then. McTavish's problem was not an easy one, for he had to find the bombing range from an obscured height. From time to time he questioned Bob about the height and speed of the aircraft.

"In a moment now we'll be turning in," said McTavish. "Right, turn in now."

Bob thought he had glimpsed the range in the distance, but was not sure and banked slightly for the spot. McTavish was flat on his stomach, watching the holes in the clouds.

"Opening bomb doors," said Bob as he pushed the hydraulic button.

"Right, sir," said McTavish, "steady."

Bob held his course and in a moment heard the sergeant's voice saying, "Bombs gone."

The craft was now noticeably lightened and Bob opened the throttle and closed the bomb doors.

"It could be a better day for it, sir," said McTavish, "but I think they dropped in the right county."

Within an hour they had completed their cross-country flight and the Stratohawk's wheels were touching the runway. The trip had gone off very well, and Bob was glad that he had drawn Don for his second pilot and McTavish for navigator. Aside from enemy aircraft and anti-aircraft fire, it was unlikely that they would ever have to find a target under more difficult conditions than those of today, and yet they had found the range on the very first run.

"Wing Commander Cranbourne would like to see you in his office, sir," said the Flight Sergeant at the hangar, "and you too, Mr. White."

Eric Prentiss was talking to Wing Commander Cranbourne as they came in.

"Sit down, boys," the Wing Commander said. "I have some news for you. I've just received word that you chaps have been officially credited with three victories on the east coast when you flew up to Edin-burgh, and that you, Terrell, have been cited for your part in that battleship show awhile back. You'll be seeing it in the *Gazette* a little later on. Appar-ently your strafing of the decks diverted the enemy's attention from a torpedo attack that crippled the ship. Unfortunately, it did not stop her. Thought I'd let you chaps know."

"Congratulations, Bob," said Eric cordially. "You took an awful chance on that show."

"To tell you the truth," admitted Bob, "I didn't know what else to do. I think they're making an awful lot out of nothing."

"Anyway," said Don, "it's nice to know that I have a good captain."

That evening the Wing Commander again ad-dressed the assembled pilots.

"According to the Met Office, tomorrow will be bright and clear with unlimited ceiling, so we're go-ing to try out a little substratosphere bombing. I think we're just about ready now to put on a show. Pilots for the first raid will be chosen according to the results of tomorrow's practice, so take your time and lay them in close."

This was the news they had been waiting for, and the room buzzed with excitement after the Wing Commander had left. Apparently the training period was nearly over.

"Well, I'm betting that Sandy lays them in just as close as any of them," said Bob. "Even today he was fairly close to the marker."

"I think most of the navigators are old-timers," interposed Roy. "My sergeant tells me he has made over fifty raids in Wellingtons and Blenheims."

"The same with mine," agreed Eric, "only his time has been spent mostly on Whitleys."

"We're lucky to have experienced air observers," said Roy, "because, boy, oh, boy, we'll surely need them. Before I joined the air force," he went on, "I'd never been any farther from home than Dallas, Texas. I sure wish I had been more studious about European geography in school. I've learned more about it in the last few weeks than I ever knew before."

"As for me," spoke up Don, "the thing I'm worried about is the air rations. See if you can't fix it up for me to get an extra amount," he asked Bob pleadingly.

"O.K., Don, I'll see what I can do," promised Bob, "but don't expect any of mine."

There was a spirit of keen competition among the assembled pilots the following morning in the bomber dispersal room, for much depended on the results of this practice bombing.

Bob, together with the Flight Sergeant, had carefully checked his Stratohawk, which had the designation "T." Don took off from the runway while Bob adjusted the pressure in the cabin. As the Met Office had predicted, the sky was practically cloudless. At fifteen thousand feet they were above the few blobs of scattered clouds. Landmarks became gradually smaller as they soared skywards.

"Thirty-five thousand now, Sandy," Bob called to McTavish as he leveled off.

"Fine, sir," replied Sandy. "What's your air speed?"

"Three twenty."

"Drop her to three hundred and hold her steady," suggested Sandy. "Now if you'll come about, sir."

The range—six miles down and many miles straight ahead—was almost invisible to Bob from this height.

"Bomb well is open, Sandy," said Bob.

"Hold it, sir."

Bob waited but Sandy McTavish made no move to drop the bombs.

"I think, sir, we'll try another run," said the cautious Sandy. "There was a wee spot of cloud got in the way."

"O.K.," said Bob and brought her around again.

"Now, sir," said Sandy, "left, left, hold it, sir." And in a moment came the "bombs gone" signal.

"I think, sir," said Sandy, "that will be adequate."

"In the county?" inquired Bob.

"Aye, sir," replied Sandy, "even in the parish."

There was something about the calm confidence of the Scotsman that inspired Bob's respect. It was not egotism; it was simply an honest belief in his own ability.

At this height there was no point in trying to see the small puffs made by their practice bombs. Bob knew that powerful glasses on the ground would identify their aircraft and check their bomb tallies.

"Take over, Don," said Bob.

"Right," replied Don with a gleam in his eye.

"Sandy," called Don over the intercom, "what

kind of flying do you like? Straight or otherwise?"

"I've tried them all, sir," replied Sandy, munching on a banana.

At just that moment the starboard engine cut off like a knife. The still roaring port engine slued them violently to the left and Don eased back on the throttle.

Bob and Don looked inquiringly at each other.

"I'd prefer, however," said McTavish as though his conversation had not been interrupted, "to do my flying with engines."

No sooner had the words left Sandy's mouth than the port engine cut out.

"Shut up, Sandy," said Bob, "or the wings will fall off."

"Aye," said Sandy calmly, continuing to munch his banana, "I wouldna be surprised. But I'm sure you've noticed that we're almost directly above the station, so a dead-stick landing should be negotiated without much difficulty."

"Thanks, Sandy," said Bob. "I hadn't noticed."

Both pilots knew that the radiotelephone was to be used only in case of greatest emergency, lest the station base be revealed to the enemy.

"Get out those flares, Don," said Sandy, "we'll need a clear runway."

Taking the flare from Don, Sandy crouched over his sights, then released the flare as they spiraled toward the runway. Down it went, and as Bob leveled off for the landing, it was burning brightly just off the runway. None too soon, either, as one of the Stratohawks had to be taxied off the runway through the grass in order to clear the way for them.

The plane bounced a bit as the wheels touched the ground, but the landing was good considering they had no power. Their plight had been seen from the ground and a tractor came down the runway to haul them in. A few minutes later they were on the hangar apron.

When Bob, Don, and Sandy crawled stiffly out of the aircraft, Wing Commander Cranbourne was waiting to meet them.

"What happened, Terrell?" he asked anxiously. "I had a telephone call from the bomb range. They saw your engines cut out, must have been around thirty thousand feet."

"I haven't the faintest idea," replied Bob. "They were functioning perfectly. The starboard engine cut out first and the port engine about one minute later. I can't figure it out, sir."

"Did you try to get them started?"

"Yes, several times," replied Bob.

"Right, sir," put in Don. "They just stopped dead."

The Wing Commander was plainly disturbed. "As you know, these planes have been carefully checked. Come inside, boys, while the Flight goes over them."

Inside, with the door closed, he continued, "Engine failures are very rare these days. It might happen with one, but two is a little bit more than a coincidence. Do you have any ideas?"

Before anyone could answer, the phone rang, and the Wing Commander jotted down figures on a chart on his desk. "I'll repeat," the boys heard him say. "That was 'R' for rhubarb, 'B' at four o'clock. That was 'S' for squash, 'C' at seven o'clock and 'T' for Terrell. 'A' at twelve o'clock. Correct?

"Well, this is good news," he said, turning back to the pilots. "Your stick fell in the center circle —dead beyond the bull's-eye. I think that counts you in on tomorrow's show without any question whatsoever."

"Tomorrow?" said the two boys inquiringly.

"Yes, tomorrow," replied the Wing Commander. "We're not going to waste any time. . . . Yes, come in," he said as the Flight Sergeant tapped discreetly on the door. "What have you found?"

"We can't find anything wrong, sir. After a quick check of the engines I tried them and they started off as fine as could be."

"I can't understand it, sir," interjected the bewildered Bob.

"Nor I," said Don.

"You chaps wait here," the Wing Commander ordered. "I want to go into this."

"I tell you, Bob," said Don after the Wing Commander had left, "that red-headed navigator is a hoodoo. Just as soon as he opened his mouth about flying, one of the engines cut out and the next time he opened his mouth, the second engine cut out. There's something wrong with any guy who would go right on eating a banana under such circumstances."

"Maybe you're the hoodoo, Don. After all, you were at the controls when it happened." But at Don's hurt look, he quickly added, "Of course you know I'm joking."

"So am I, too, in a way," admitted Don, "but there's something mighty queer about this business."

In about twenty minutes the Wing Commander returned.

"Terrell," he said, "you're captain of this ship, and as such you're responsible for anything that happens in the air. White, here, was at the controls, but you are still the captain, so I'll have to charge this little practical joke up to you—and we haven't time for practical joking around here."

"There's some mistake, sir," replied Bob flushing. "We weren't joking."

"No?" queried the Wing Commander. "Then how does it happen that the engine cut out directly after your joking conversation with McTavish?"

"That does seem to be a coincidence."

"McTavish thinks so, but I don't. He's as puzzled as you are. I was just talking to him out on the tarmac. Oh, no," he added, noting the pilot's faces, "he wasn't telling tales out of school. It so happens that McTavish is one of the best navigators in the Air Force. I ought to know; I had him for quite a while myself and I resent this practical joke on him more than anything else."

"But, sir," protested Bob. "Please believe me; it was no joke."

"In that case," said the Wing Commander, "we'll have to declare your aircraft unserviceable and you know what that means."

"Yes, sir," said Bob weakly. "It means that we'll be out of the raid tomorrow."

"I'm afraid it does," replied the Wing Commander, noticing the keen look of disappointment on the pilots' faces.

Don, Bob and Sandy felt completely out of things as they gathered with the others in the Briefing Room in preparation for the next day's raid. McTavish was just as disappointed as Bob and Don.

The raid, as Roy Benson had predicted, was to be against a Nazi air base in Norway, one of the large airdromes being used by the Luftwaffe. The lights went out in the Briefing Room and the Intelligence Officer screened photographs of the airdrome made by R.A.F. observation planes.

"This is a Focke-Wulf field and a base for use against our North Sea shipping," explained the Intelligence Officer. "Recently the raids have been intensified and we're hoping to reach there in time to catch the morning patrol planes when they start off the runway. Our reports indicate that the usual take-off time is seven A.M. A five A.M. departure should give us ample time to reach the objective."

Bob and Don, feeling completely useless as the pilots and navigators huddled together over their maps and photographs, decided to go to bed. Puzzled, as well as disappointed, Bob could not sleep, and when Eric came in they talked over what had happened.

"You know, Bob," said Eric, "I've been thinking about those engines cutting out like they did. There's something funny about that. Do you suppose it might have been supercharger trouble? At that height the air is so rare and the temperature so low and you'd been up there quite awhile when it happened."

"No," said Bob, "I don't think so. They checked over everything at the hangar. But wait a minute. Temperature—that gives me an idea."

"What's that?" asked Eric. "What else would the temperature have to do with it?"

"I'm really not sure," replied Bob slowly, "but I just recalled something that I heard a while back. Could it possibly have any connection?"

"What on earth are you talking about?" asked Eric, looking at him quizzically.

"Oh, nothing, really, but I wonder if it's too late to see Wing Commander Cranbourne tonight?"

"You must be crazy," said Eric. "Anyway, he's off the station and he won't be back until morning. He's going on the raid, you know."

Another hour passed before Bob finally drifted off into a troubled sleep.

CHAPTER VIII

Sabotage!

"I say, Terrell, what are you doing here?" asked the C.O. as he saw Bob on the tarmac the next morning.

"I know I'm not in on this show, sir, but I wanted to have a word with you before you take off. You asked me yesterday what might be wrong with the Stratohawk, and now I have an idea what it is. It may not be worth anything, but I'd like to try it out."

"What kind of idea?" asked the Wing Commander.

"I'd like to check the plane thoroughly myself, sir," said Bob, "with the Flight Sergeant, and I'd like to start just as quickly as possible."

"All right, Terrell, go ahead." He called to the Flight Sergeant. "See that Mr. Terrell gets all the help he wants in checking over his plane today, will you, Flight?"

"Gladly, sir," replied the Flight Sergeant.

For almost an hour, he and the Flight Sergeant, with two aircraftmen, troubleshot the plane.

"It's got me stumped," declared the Flight Sergeant after their thorough examination.

"Let's warm up the engines and let them run for a little while anyway," said Bob, "just in case the Wing Commander sends for reinforcements."

Just as Bob slipped the port engine's ignition switches he noticed a small scratch over one of the panel screwheads. That was strange, for the panel was sprayed after the screws were inserted. Evidently someone had removed this section of the panel recently. Taking a small screw driver from the emergency kit, Bob opened the panel section, which left an opening large enough to insert the hand.

Meanwhile, the Flight Sergeant had walked back into the hangar. So as not to excite his curiosity, Bob threw the switches and started the engines. They functioned perfectly and, while they were ticking over, Bob examined the wiring behind the switches of the port engine. A wire from each had been bared and the insulation cut off. Tiny clamps, similar to those used on storage battery connectors, were attached to each bared wire and between the clamps was a small boxlike affair about the size of a penny matchbox. Gingerly, with engines still running, Bob depressed the clamps, lifted out the gadget, and hurriedly replaced the panel. All this time the engines continued to tick over smoothly.

Seething with excitement, but not wishing to show undue haste, Bob slowly left the plane.

"Giving up, sir?" asked the Flight Sergeant as he came out of the hangar.

"Not exactly giving up," answered Bob, "but I think I'll go back to quarters for awhile."

As soon as he was clear of the hangar, Bob fairly ran towards quarters.

"Squadron Leader Anderson was very explicit about not being disturbed," said Anderson's batman, when Bob asked for the Chief Intelligence Officer, "but if you insist, sir, I'll call him."

"I'll call him myself," said Bob, rapping loudly on his door.

"Come in, come in," said a gruff voice, and Bob entered to find the Squadron Leader sitting up in bed.

"Good heavens, Terrell, don't you know I've been

up all night working on this raid and wasn't even able to get to bed until the squadron took off?"

"Yes, sir, I do know," said Terrell, "and I'm awfully sorry to disturb you, but this is vitally important."

"Well, out with it then."

Bob related the previous day's experiences, telling of the engine failures and the aircraftmen's inability to find the cause.

"Yes, yes, I know all about that, Terrell, but what has that to do with waking me up now?"

"Well, sir, I think perhaps I've found the reason, and if I have, the whole squadron may be endangered on its flight to Norway."

"Good heavens, what are you saying, man?" Squadron Leader Anderson sprang out of bed.

"I found this, sir," Terrell said, pulling the gadget out of his pocket, "behind my instrument panel fastened between the magneto lead wires from the main switch. I don't know how it works, but I'm wondering if it might not be by metal contraction. You know the temperatures are fifty and more below zero in the substratosphere. That's where my engine failed yesterday."

"To save time, Terrell, go find Flight Lieutenant Kelly at once and bring him here—and hurry. If what you say is true, we've no time to waste. Kelly knows those engines inside and out."

Kelly was in bed, too, but he dressed hurriedly and in less than five minutes they were back in Squadron Leader Anderson's room.

"Kelly," began Anderson, "you know these Strato-hawk engines. What does this gadget have to do with the ignition system?"

Kelly examined it closely. "Nothing at all, sir '

"Terrell found it clamped behind his magneto switches. As you know, both his engines failed yesterday and he has an idea that it may be some kind of metal contraction switch."

"I believe you're right, Terrell," said Kelly, "but there's no way of testing it now. Let's open it up and see what it looks like."

Inside was a peculiar springlike arrangement so devised that when the spring contracted, contact would be established.

"You've hit it on the head, Terrell," admitted Anderson. "There isn't a minute to lose. This fiendish contrivance was designed to short the engine and there's likely one behind the switches for the other engine. Don't say a word about this or let on that you've discovered the trouble with your plane. Go directly to the operations room and I'll join you there in a moment."

It was now nearly seven o'clock—the time set for the attack on the enemy airdrome, the time at which the planes would be at their greatest height. Squadron Leader Anderson soon appeared with a paper in hand.

"Come with me, Terrell." He gave the message to the duty officer with the instructions, "This is to be sent in code to Wing Commander Cranbourne at once. Keep trying until you get him, for he must have this message."

They followed the duty officer into the wireless room and in a few moments the call letters were going out over the air. They were repeated again and again, followed by instructions to stand by for a coded message. Each minute seemed like an hour to Bob and Squadron Leader Anderson, but finally the wireless keys were crackling out the coded warning.

"The trouble is," said Anderson, "we'll get no

acknowledgment, and we won't know whether the message got through or not. Any reply would give away the squadron's position to the enemy. All we can hope is that the message arrives in time, but I very much doubt it."

"It's probable," the Met Officer interposed, "that they've been held up by head winds crossing the North Sea."

"Let's hope so," said Bob. "As I figure it, they'll be perfectly safe until they get into the substratosphere, or at least until they've reached an altitude where the temperature is very low.

"I think that the low temperature is the basic principle of this device," he continued. "The saboteurs evidently figure that the Stratohawks will be up in substratosphere only when they are over the North Sea or over enemy territory. In either case, it would mean loss of planes and the possibility of their falling into enemy hands."

"I only hope," said Anderson fervently, "that if anyone does come down over Norway he will remember the demolition switch. It would be disastrous if one of these planes got into the hands of the enemy now."

"We might as well go over to the mess," said Anderson, "and have a cup of coffee and a bite to eat. It will be at least two hours before we know whether or not the message got through in time.

"I can't understand," Anderson continued, when their coffee had been served, "how this could have happened. Every man on the station was picked for this work with the greatest care. No one except the Wing Commander and a few of us in the Intelligence Department even know the exact location of the station. All mail is sent up from Edinburgh by train so that it isn't possible for anyone to direct a letter or a package here. There is one thing certain: these gadgets were not made on the station. They've been imported."

"Don't you think," suggested Bob, "that it would be a good idea for me to go back to the hangar and tinker around my plane as if I were still trying to find the trouble? It might ward off suspicion if someone in the ground crew is responsible. It's likely that my engine failures weren't intended to take place yesterday, but on the first raid."

"Yes," agreed Anderson, "I think that's a good idea. If I were you, I'd carry the idea just a bit further and take the Stratohawk up for a flip a little later on."

When Bob reached the hangar, the Flight Sergeant was just climbing out from the belly door of the Stratohawk.

"This thing still has me stumped, sir," he said to Bob. "It just occurred to me there might be something wrong with the switches and so I've looked at the port engine switch, but it seems to be absolutely O.K."

Bob felt that this remark put the Flight Sergeant in the clear. If he were responsible, he would not have m̲ ̲ ̲ ̲oned the switches.

"I think, Flight, that if you'll have her refueled, I'll take her up a little later on. I'll go up and get Mr. White now."

Fifteen minutes later, Bob, Don, and Sandy were in the air.

"I thought, Bob," said Don, "that Wing Commander Cranbourne had declared this ship unserviceable."

"That's true," admitted Bob, "but I saw him before the take-off this morning and he gave me permission to see if I could find out what is wrong. Later I'll

rell. "We'll have to get those switches out of the aircraft."

"We certainly will," agreed the Wing Commander. "Of course it's possible that all the planes haven't been tampered with, but we must be sure. Come in and see me after lunch and in the meantime I'll try to figure out a plan."

Bob hurried into the lounge and talked with Eric and Roy about the morning raid. Everyone had assumed that the missing planes had been shot down by anti-aircraft fire, but no one understood why the Wing Commander had changed orders at the last moment for a low level attack on the airdrome.

"It was certainly a hot spot," said Roy, "but we made a mess of that Nazi airfield."

"Let's hear about it," suggested Bob.

"Well," began Eric, "it was like this. We were still climbing for altitude at thirty-two thousand when the orders were changed. Radio silence had been ordered, so naturally I was surprised. Cranbourne led us down to ten thousand feet. As we ran in, there were six Focke-Wulf planes bunched at the end of the runway, apparently waiting to take off.

The Wing Commander straddled them with a stick and I don't think there's anything left of them at all. My target was a repair hangar and Smythe, my navigator, says we made a direct hit, although I didn't see it myself."

"We were assigned a fuel storage tank, which we missed," said Roy. "But we did get three Focke-Wulf ships that were lined up near by for refueling."

"We got the fuel tanks, Benson," said Barker, another pilot who joined the group. "So don't worry about them."

"Altogether it sounds as though the raid had been successful in spite of the losses," said Bob. "I certainly wish I could have been in on it."

"I wish you had, too," agreed Eric. "Have you found out what's wrong with your kite?"

"She was fine when I took her up this morning," answered Bob, "and I'm to see the Wing Commander after lunch."

"You'll be in on the next show all right," said Roy.

"That's what I'm figuring on," said Bob soberly.

When Bob returned to the Commanding Officer's office after lunch, Cranbourne was talking with nine other pilots, including Eric and Roy.

"We all must thank Terrell for our separate skins," he was saying as Bob entered, "for he has uncovered a diabolical attempt at sabotage. That is why your attack orders were changed this morning. He managed to get in touch with me by radio. The squadron will be off on another raid tomorrow. I'm telling you chaps about it, but no one else is to know."

Then he explained about Bob's discovery of the switch.

"I'm sending you each off on practice hops this afternoon. When you are out of sight of the hangar and before you take off at the end of the runway, be sure to remove the switches, if any, in your aircraft. Tell them how to do it, Terrell."

Bob quickly explained how the panel could be removed and the switch detached.

"All right, gentlemen, that is all," said the Wing Commander when Bob had concluded, "and remember, not a word of this to anyone. Your copilots, of course, will have to know, but it must not go any further."

Bob found another switch behind his starboard engine, and Eric found two in his aircraft. Roy, however, found none, so apparently the saboteur had not tampered with all the planes. The balance of the day was spent in preparation for their target of the morrow. It was one of the most difficult of them all—a great naval base in north Germany. For all they knew, the escaped German cruisers or battleships might be berthed there now.

"This type of objective," explained the Briefing Officer to the assembled pilots late that afternoon, "should be made to order for the Stratohawk. Because your targets are enemy naval vessels and the dock and wharfage installations around them, a high level attack is out of the question. We have reports that several of the large battleships are ready to put to sea, which makes it vital for us to immobilize them. That will be your job. Weather predictions are good and you should have no difficulty in finding your targets. Your secondary or alternative target will be the same airdrome you bombed this morning."

At the end of the briefing lecture, which lasted half an hour, Bob, Don, and Sandy poured over the various photographs and maps that would familiarize them with the targets.

"Aye, it's a bonnie spot, this," said Sandy as they

examined a large-scale photograph, "and it looks much the same as when I was last over it."

"Oh, you're familiar with this objective?" asked Bob.

"Aye," said Sandy, "I feel very much at home there." Then he went into great detail about the names and locations of the various ships berthed at the dock.

"That will be the one assigned to ourselves and Mr. Benson," said Sandy, pointing to one of the larger ships in the picture.

The ships were long and narrow and Bob realized that critical sighting would be required in order to score hits.

"Our main trouble will be the flak," went on Sandy. "Unless, sir, you'd feel like coming in a bit low."

"That's what I'd like to do," agreed Bob. "Here's hoping that it works out that way."

"Altogether," said Sandy, "it sounds like a most promising trip, and," he added, looking at Don, "if I may say so, sir, a rather hungry one, too."

CHAPTER IX

Stratohawk versus Heinkel

It seemed to Bob that he hardly had fallen asleep that night when he heard a compelling knock on his door.

"Four-thirty, gentlemen," said the batman. "All out."

Bob and Eric immediately jumped out of bed. As he scrambled into his clothes, Bob realized that this would be a long patrol and a cold one. Over his silk socks he pulled heavy woolen stockings and then flying boots lined with lamb's wool. The two boys slipped on sweaters over their uniforms and then, picking up their flying suits and helmets, started for the mess hall.

There was not much conversation among the twelve pilots during their hurried breakfast. Wing Commander Cranbourne was waiting for them in the dispersal room.

"Sorry I can't go with you, but something has come up to detain me here. Flight Lieutenant Osborne will be in charge. You're all familiar with the plan. Good luck, and lay them in there close."

When the Wing Commander had left, pilots and copilots got together with their navigators and worked out their course in detail. Each plane was to be on its own from start to finish, although Flight Lieutenant Osborne was in charge in case his assistance was required. There were brief messages from the Meteorological Officer and the Armaments Officer. All planes were carrying heavy demolition bombs, and Flight Lieutenant Osborne's aircraft was also carrying a camera. He would make the last run.

As they left the dispersal room, each was handed his bag of rations for the flight. Pilots and navigators were crowded into the lorry, and a few minutes later were at the airfield. In the half-light, Bob could see that the Stratohawks had been widely dispersed over the field.

"Go ahead," said Bob to Don. "You next, Sandy."

The navigator scrambled on board. He was carrying a green canvas satchel. Inside were the tools of his trade: colored pencils, dividers, a protractor, the course speed calculator, a log book, and a target map. There was also the questionnaire to be filled in for the Met Officer, so that weather conditions could be checked, and the Astro Navigation tables by which Sandy would guide them so long as the stars were visible.

As Bob squeezed in behind the controls, Don was calling the station.

"Hello, Carrot, hello, Carrot. 'T' for Terrell calling, 'T' for Terrell calling. Are you receiving me, are you receiving me? Over to you, over to you."

The watch office acknowledged Don's message and told him his signals were loud and clear.

The planes already had been fueled and bombed up. The runway was perfectly clear under a peculiar method of lighting which Bob knew made it invisible to anyone more than five hundred feet above. They were taking off at one-minute intervals, and Bob anxiously awaited the green flare. His plane was scheduled as the fifth to leave.

Soon the aircraft ahead of him roared down the runway. He was next. The seconds ticked off. Then came the flash, and he gave the gun to his heavily burdened plane. In spite of the heavy load, the Stratohawk took to the air after a very short run, and in a few moments they were at a thousand feet.

"Hello, sir," said Sandy, "the course is X degree."

Turning in, Bob was soon on course and so reported to Sandy. It was more than five hundred miles to their objective, and once beyond the Scottish coast, they would fly over water until they reached the target. Nothing more was heard from Sandy until they reached the coast, when he gave Bob a flight correction in course bearing.

"O.K., Sandy. I'm going up to ten thousand and will hold it at three hundred."

For at least an hour and a half they would be flying over the North Sea. A few scattered clouds were breasted on the way up to the assigned flight level. The course was almost due southeast, and as the sun came up, the stars quickly faded away. A flow of light was filtering through the low-hanging clouds on the horizon, but soon it became a yellow-orange ball, a dazzling nuisance over the port wing.

"That doesn't look very good to me," said Don. "I hope we'll have more cover than this over the target."

"The Met people are usually right," answered Bob, "and they predicted clouds. Anyway, I think we'd better get some more height. We're going up, Sandy."

"Aye," said Sandy, "I think it's a wise move. We'll be in their patrol area any time now."

Bob called off the height to Sandy as they climbed, and at thirty thousand they leveled off.

"Just about now we'd be doing a swan dive if you hadn't found those switches," remarked Don.

"That's right," agreed Bob. "I think maybe that's the reason the skipper stayed behind this morning. He's probably doing some investigating."

About ten thousand feet beneath them there was a tightly packed cloud layer.

"I wonder how far down it goes," mused Bob.

"We'll soon know," answered Don, adding quickly, "Aircraft to starboard."

The plane was too far away for identification, but they all hoped it was one of their own.

"I'd hate to tangle with anyone until we get rid of these bombs," Bob said thoughtfully.

"Bombs are live now, sir," reported Sandy, "and I believe another five minutes on this course will just about do it."

Don was now able to identify the aircraft as one

of their own, and as he watched, it dropped down towards the clouds and a few moments later was lost to view.

"That seems to confirm Sandy's reckonings," said Bob.

At the end of the five-minute period Bob eased off on his throttle and began to glide down toward the white cloud banks beneath.

"All I'll need," said Sandy, "is a quick glimpse once we're below them, and then you can pull up again and we'll make our run."

For what seemed an endless period, they kept dropping through the seething mass. The moisture was whipping by even at five thousand feet, but it seemed to be thinning. Bob had been dropping in wide, lazy spirals, clearing his engines at intervals.

Sandy lay flat on his belly on the floor, and at four thousand feet he called excitedly, "Hold it there, sir."

Bob straightened out and continued the gliding descent.

"Thirty-eight hundred," he called out to the navigator.

"Good. Give her the gun. I think she'll be dead ahead."

Bob opened the bomb wells and poured in the power. Now he and Don could see the naval base through thin wisps of clouds, while some distance ahead were the great docks. Quickly he looked for their target, the huge aircraft carrier under construction.

"A thousand," Sandy called to Bob.

"A thousand," Bob replied.

With full engines the Stratohawk roared relentlessly toward the target, which was still several miles away. Perfect bedlam had broken out on the ground below. Even at their terrific speed Bob could see it clearly. People scurried from the open streets, and flashes of fire dotted the ground where anti-aircraft units were pouring flak skywards. Would they run through a barrage of ground fire, or had they taken the enemy by surprise? In seconds now, they would be on their target.

At lightning speed the huge aircraft carrier lying in the dock seemed to come rocketing toward them. Bob could see the workmen scrambling like ants for cover.

"Bombs gone," said Sandy, as the bow of the carrier shot beneath the nose of the plane.

Immediately Bob banked to escape the tremendous concussion that he knew must follow. Then the Stratohawk swerved dizzily as Bob climbed for the shelter of the clouds. A moment later, even above the roaring of the engines, they could hear a dull-throated blast. Flak was shooting up from the ground. It streaked and shrieked around them, alarmingly near.

"Sandy," called Bob, "I'm going down again. There isn't enough room for Osborne to get pictures and we'll have to know how much damage has been done."

"Aye," said Sandy, "but I'd suggest the opposite way. They'll not be expecting you from that direction."

"Fine," said Bob.

Banking widely, he brought the Stratohawk around, and then standing her almost on her nose, bored down through the clouds. But Bob had misjudged it slightly, and as they emerged below the clouds, the aircraft carrier lay somewhat ahead and off to starboard. Smoke was pouring from a great jagged hole in the forward part of her deck. Sandy had scored a direct hit.

"You've gone and got her," called Don exultantly.

"Aye," said Sandy, "but would you mind pulling over a bit closer, Mr. Terrell, so I can have a better look?"

Bob dove for the carrier, then pulled up so that Sandy could look through the glass bottom of the plane. A mass of fire came at them from the ground, and Bob could feel the jarring as hits scored. None of them seemed to affect the Stratohawk, and in a few moments they had gained the safety of the clouds.

"I was afraid of that," said Sandy. "A wee bit short."

"Shucks," said Don. "Where did you expect to put it?"

"Well, I had hoped," replied Sandy, "to lay it in a bit closer amidships. It would take longer to repair there."

"It looks to me," said Don, "as if it would take plenty long to repair it now. Nice shooting, Sandy."

"I think that we'd better stick around in these clouds for awhile," suggested Bob. "They'll likely have a pretty hot reception committee waiting for us up on top."

"What is your course now, sir?" asked Sandy.

Bob gave the course.

"Just a wee bit more to starboard and that'll bring us out about right."

Bob shifted the course as directed and ploughed along steadily through the clouds.

"Take over for awhile, will you, Don? I think I'll have some lunch."

"Jumping catfish!" exclaimed Don. "I'd forgotten all about it. Hurry up, Bob."

"O.K.," laughed Bob as he took over the controls again. "You'd better go to it now because we may not have a chance to eat when we get out into the clear. I wouldn't be surprised if the Jerries came at us from all directions."

Hurriedly wolfing his way through a couple of sandwiches, Don poured some coffee for himself and Bob. The clouds had thinned somewhat, and at eighteen thousand feet they emerged in the clear, with only a few scattered clouds above.

"Keep an eye open there below, will you, Sandy?" asked Bob.

Bob scanned the horizon, but there was no evidence of aircraft ahead or to either side of them.

"Looks like an uneventful trip, Bob," said Don, now nearing the bottom of his ration bag.

The words hardly had been spoken when Sandy called out sharply, "Aircraft dead astern, sir, and coming up fast."

Bob heeled the plane over into a steep bank and scanned the space beneath. Sure enough, there were six new fast Heinkel fighters. As he pulled up for more altitude, they split into two sections of three each, endeavoring to box him in, but Bob's quick maneuver had spoiled their plans. The guns of the lead plane of one section were blazing as it passed swiftly beneath.

Both sections of Heinkels were now climbing quickly to cut him off. There was no cover and no chance of making a run for it, at least not at this altitude. Now was the glorious opportunity to see what the Stratohawk would do, for this Heinkel was supposed to be Jerry's fastest fighter.

At any moment the first section would be around on Bob's tail again, but the other was still climbing squarely ahead. Appraising the situation in a split second, Bob glued his ring full on the lead plane in that climbing "V." It would have been a hopeless shot for a Spitfire, equipped only with machine guns, but the four cannon of the Stratohawk might do it. Squeezing the button, he felt the jolt of the twenty-millimeter shells as they streamed forth. The shells caught the Heinkel squarely in the fuselage. Where there had been a tail a split second before, now there was none.

The two following Heinkels dodged wildly to miss their leader as he nosed down toward the earth, leaving them to their own resources. Bob banked swiftly to port, and out of the corner of his eye saw the other section of three Heinkels turning toward him. Once more he had wiggled out of the trap. Guns were blazing as they flashed by. Shoving the Stratohawk's nose up, Bob climbed for altitude. Now all five Heinkels were after him, but still beyond range. At twenty-five thousand they had made no appreciable gain.

Easing back ever so slightly on the throttle, Bob saw the distance between them shorten. At thirty thousand feet they were almost within range and Bob poured in more power.

"In case you might wish to use it, sir," said Sandy through the intercom, "there's a beautiful layer of clouds about ten miles off to the north and at about fifteen thousand feet."

"Thanks, Sandy," replied Bob. "I'll edge over that way."

The Heinkels, apparently feeling sure of their quarry, were spreading out a bit to close in. Although he had complete confidence in the Strato-hawk, Bob was beginning to wonder whether or not he was doing the wise thing. Good as his own plane was, this new job of Jerry's might possibly be a little better. Still climbing, he began to edge over slightly toward the cloud banks. At thirty-five thousand feet the Heinkels were still following. Bob had long since put the pressure system into operation. At thirty-eight thousand they were still coming.

"It won't be long now," said Don, "before we know who's really building the best airplanes."

The two leaderless Heinkels were no longer in sight; only the section of three was hanging on. There seemed to be no horizon now at all; land, sea, and sky were all mixed in together. The sky was no longer the familiar blue dome as seen from below. Everything now was darker, as though they were flying in a huge fish bowl filled with smoke.

Then Bob saw that the leader's guns were blazing, and at the same moment he felt the impact of shells. Ruddering sharply to avoid the fire, he was startled at the lack of response. Was it the thin air, or had they caught the rudder? Using the ailerons, he banked over steeply. As he did so, he saw the Heinkels turn and dart downwards. Now, directly on their tails, he opened fire. The altimeter registered forty-three thousand feet as he turned earthward. Engines screamed as he tore after the Heinkels, now escaping in a smoky haze. Not really sure whether they were in range or not, Bob squeezed the button. With a feeling of detached surprise, he saw one of the Heinkels, full in his sights, burst into flames, while the other two disappeared into the clouds beneath.

Pulling up gradually from the terrific dive, Bob found that the controls functioned almost normally in the heavier air at fifteen thousand feet.

"Want to take her over a bit?" he asked Don.

"You know, Bob," said Don, forgetting to cut off the intercom system, "I think perhaps that's as close as I'll ever get to heaven."

"I wouldna be surprised, sir," spoke up Sandy dourly.

The sun was high in the sky when Bob set the Stratohawk's wheels on the runway at the base in Scotland. The trip home had been uneventful after their encounter with the Heinkels, and the three boys clambered stiffly out of their cramped quarters as the Stratohawk came to a halt on the tarmac.

"My stomach," said Don, "says that it's after lunch-time, but my watch says it isn't quite eleven o'clock."

"I'll bet that's the first time you ever put in nearly fifteen hundred miles between breakfast and lunch," remarked Bob.

"You're the first in, sir," said the Flight Sergeant to Bob as a tractor was attached to the plane and hauled it away for servicing.

"Are we? I thought we'd be the last."

"Come into the office for a minute, boys," said Wing Commander Cranbourne as they were making out their reports. "We've had no word yet from the other aircraft. Did you see anything of them?"

Bob told of the one aircraft that had disappeared into the clouds just before he had made his run. "But I saw nothing more of him, sir."

"Well, McTavish," went on the Wing Commander, "I hear that you made a direct hit."

"Aye," said Sandy, "but it could have been better."

"Better?" echoed Bob. "Why, there was a hole as big as this room right in the middle of the carrier's deck."

"That's fine," praised Cranbourne, "but I wonder about the others?"

"I think, sir," offered Sandy, "that they went on to the secondary target. It was only a matter of extreme good fortune that we found this target."

"Well, I hope that's the case," said the Wing Commander, "and if so, we ought to be hearing from them soon. I see, boys, that you got mixed up with some of the new Heinkels."

"Yes, sir," said Bob, "but they're not quite as good as they're reported to be."

"So I gather from the combat reports."

"If I may say so, sir," interjected Sandy, "it was a bonnie bit of flying that Mr. Terrell did. I can confirm that one of the Heinkels went home without his tail and the second was in flames as he entered the clouds."

"Nice work, Terrell," said Wing Commander Cranbourne enthusiastically. "This report is going to interest the Bomber Command immensely, because it will be the first report on combat with the enemy's new Heinkels and we weren't too sure which aircraft had the greater ceiling."

Just then the telephone rang and the Wing Commander was advised that some of the other aircraft were returning.

"I'd like to have a few more words with you, Mr. Terrell," he said as he left the office, "so please wait here. I'll be back in a few minutes."

Don and Sandy left. Bob waited impatiently, for he was anxious about the safe return of Eric and Roy.

"We've been working hard on this switch business," began the Wing Commander when he returned, "but so far nothing has developed. The Command now has full details of the incident. The trouble is that so many aircraftmen had access to the planes. Any one of them could have inserted the switches. Whoever was responsible must now know that his plan isn't working out a hundred per cent. By the way," he added, "your friends Prentiss and Benson have just returned.

"Would you mind repeating that conversation about the switch that you overheard in the restaurant in London? I don't quite see the significance as yet."

As well as he could remember it, Bob repeated what he had heard. "I don't think there's any particular significance, sir, except as it suggested that particular kind of sabotage to me."

"I see," said the Wing Commander thoughtfully. "Certainly we wouldn't have much to go on there. Do you think you'd recognize these men if you saw them again?"

"Yes, I think so."

"Well, we're checking on that angle. I'll let you know if anything develops. In the meantime, some new aircraftmen have been added at the hangar for the express purpose of keeping their eyes open. New aircraft will be arriving soon and more pilots to man them. Someone, we believe, will attempt to tamper with the new planes. Congratulations on this raid today, Terrell, and the best of luck for the future."

"Thank you, sir."

Bob found Don over in the mess, and in a few moments they were joined by Eric and Roy.

"Say, what happened to you birds?" asked Don.

"It was so thick over that Jerry naval base," said Roy, "that we went on up to Norway."

"Same here," said Eric.

"You fellows ought to have a good navigator like Sandy," boasted Bob pridefully. "We got right to the target."

"Too bad you didn't come up to Norway," said Roy. "You should have seen that Luftwaffe base. I had no idea how much damage we did yesterday until I had a good look at it today. There's nothing left of the repair hangar that Eric hit except the framework, and the field is strewn with Focke-Wulf skeletons."

"And from the way the runways are ploughed up," elaborated Eric, "it's going to be some time before they can use the airdrome, let alone get in new aircraft."

"I understand," said Eric, "that you fellows ran

into some Heinkels today, some of the new type."

"Yes," said Don, "it was like this. I was just starting a sandwich when out of the corner of my eye, over the starboard wing, I saw about two hundred and fifty Heinkels coming up at us. So I finished my sandwich, and then said to Bob, 'Captain, there are several hundred Heinkels approaching from starboard.' And the captain replied, 'Do tell.' Sandy, the navigator, suggested that we continue on course until he had finished his lunch. So we continued northwest at an altitude of fifty thousand feet, and——"

"Oh, shut up, Don," said Roy, "give us the real dope, Terrell."

Bob told them how the Stratohawk had behaved in the thin air around forty thousand feet. Eric and Roy were intensely interested and full of congratulations for Bob.

"And," said Eric, "you got two Heinkels, I understand."

"Well," admitted Bob, "we can't be sure, but I think so."

"Better let me continue the story, Bob," broke in Don, "in my own inimitable way." But he dropped his foolishness and gave an accurate account of the combat, ending, "and my captain did a bonnie bit of flying."

"I think," said Bob, embarrassed at their praise, "that if you'll excuse me, I'll go down to the hangar and see how much damage 'T' for Terrell has suffered. I know that we picked up a few slugs."

"Bob," began Don seriously as they approached the hangar, "I have a confession to make. You know how it is when you're used to driving a car yourself and then sometimes you're not in the driver's seat. First thing you know, you find yourself pressing down on the floor boards when the car comes to a stop. Well, I have to admit that I felt a little bit that way during that brush with the Heinkels. But I wanted you to know that I don't have that feeling any longer. From now on, boy, I'm perfectly happy to sit back and let you hang onto the controls."

"Thanks, Don," said Bob. "I know exactly how you felt, and I'd have felt the same way. You had the hardest job—sitting back there and wondering what I'd be doing next."

"It's funny," explained Don, "but I wasn't doing

much wondering. As a matter of fact, I seemed to be doing what you were doing all the time. As soon as you pulled out of that first attack, I was flying right with you. I think it comes from our flying together so much on fighter patrols."

"That's probably it," agreed Bob, "and I'm sure that I would feel exactly the same if you had been at the controls."

Actually, very little damage had been done to the Stratohawk. The rudder had been shot up a bit, which accounted for some of the lack of control at the higher altitudes. Repairs were going ahead quickly, and the Flight Sergeant assured Bob that it would be ready for service the following day if needed.

As the boys were leaving the hangar, the last two aircraft came in: Flight Lieutenant Osborne with the camera equipment and Flying Officer Mitchell, who had finally found the naval base and had successfully bombed his target. Osborne's aircraft, however, was badly shot up.

"I think," said Osborne, "that, in spite of the low ceiling, we got some good pictures. That was a swell job you did on that aircraft carrier, Terrell.

That baby will be out of commission for a long
time to come, and from all appearances she was almost ready to slide down the ways."

That night the pilots congregated in the lounge
after dinner while Squadron Leader Anderson
showed them photographs of the damage done to
the enemy naval base and the Luftwaffe airdrome
in Norway. Wing Commander Cranbourne was
delighted with the results of the raid and told the
assembled pilots of his satisfaction. There were no
adverse comments for those who had failed to find
their objectives.

"It was a difficult assignment," concluded Cranbourne, "under the weather conditions that developed. Far better to go on to your secondary target,
as some of you did, when you can't make an effec-
tive run on the first. Every bomb must count."

The pilots congratulated Bob enthusiastically, for
the photographs showed clearly that the aircraft
carrier had been seriously damaged. Bob and Don
were naturally pleased with the Wing Commander's
praise. They had been advised to stand by for another raid on the following day, but weather conditions were uncertain and Anderson indicated that

he thought there was little chance that it would come off.

Actually, it was to be many days before the boys took to the air again, and they anxiously waited for the weather to clear.

CHAPTER X

HAPPY LANDING!

GROUND classes were now spaced far enough apart so that Bob had a chance to catch up with his correspondence. Since America was now at war letters from home took on added significance. Many of his friends had entered the army or navy, and Bob wondered how America's participation might affect his own future. He had never regretted leaving Texas and joining the Royal Canadian Air Force. Now the day might soon come when he would be flying side by side with the air services of his own country. He might even be transferred to one of them.

"I'm certainly getting fed up on this weather," said Roy Benson as they were waiting for mess call one evening, "but I understand from the Met Office that it's going to lift soon."

Just then an orderly came up to post a notice on the bulletin board.

"It looks like action, fellows," said Don, reading

the notice. "The Wing Commander has called a meeting of pilots after dinner tonight."

"I wonder what will be next," mused Bob.

"I know that you chaps are getting rather impatient with this inactivity," began Wing Commander Cranbourne when they had gathered in the lounge, "but I think I have some good news for you. The Met Office advises that tomorrow night ought to be an ideal time for a raid on Berlin."

The lounge rang with cheers from the assembled pilots, who now numbered nearly a hundred.

"We are planning," continued the Wing Commander, smiling at their enthusiasm, "to send three full squadrons on this show. It will be the greatest test yet for the Stratohawks and for yourselves, but I haven't any doubt that you'll both do a fine job. Mr. Anderson will go into details about your targets, for we're going after specific ones and not just to put the wind up among the citizens of the German capital. But," he added, "if our attack is successful, we will accomplish that objective also. Squadron Leader Anderson will now give you some details of the plan and tomorrow we will spend most of the day in a careful study of the situation, particularly of the recent attempts at camouflage on the part of the Jerries."

Photographs were then thrown on the screen and a discussion of the pictures, along with the Squadron Leader's talk, lasted over an hour. It reminded Bob of classroom lectures during his first year in college, but never in college had he seen such rapt attention. Every pilot knew that the success of the raid depended upon a thorough knowledge of the situation. In fact, the safe return of himself, his air crew, and his aircraft were all at ʌʌ̣ʌ̣c.

"You will, of course," warned Anderson, "run into plenty of opposition. The flak around these vital objectives is particularly heavy, and German night fighters are appearing in increasing number. They seem to have caught on to our successful night tactics pretty well. Our departure will be planned at twenty-four hours. That will give us a dark run to and from Berlin with enough light to pick up the coast line on the return so that you won't overshoot Scotland."

The boys knew this was no joke, for if the Atlantic were confused with the North Sea, the next landfall westward might be the top of North America.

"All right, fellows," said Squadron Leader Anderson, "you'd better turn in now. You'll have a heavy day tomorrow, and you'll be able to use some of that extra sleep tomorrow night."

It was some time, however, before conversation died down in the hut. The supreme desire of every pilot in the Royal Air Force was to bomb Berlin, and now they would be among those to have a chance to realize that ambition.

"Bob," said Eric softly, as both boys lay in their cots after the lights had gone out, "I was just thinking. Here we are way up in the north of Scotland. Tomorrow night we fly to Berlin, over eight hundred miles away. Allowing an hour over the target, we ought to be back here for an early breakfast. Just think of it. This war is going to bring out developments in aviation that might make it possible to fly around the world without refueling. Just think what that will mean when this war is over— if it ever is over."

"Yes," replied Bob soberly, "it can be a wonderful

world if we win." And on that note, the boys dropped off to sleep.

The next day, busy to the brim, passed quickly.

"Aye, it's a bonnie sight," said Sandy, as he and Bob and Don were plotting their course after the last-minute weather information had come in.

"What's a bonnie sight, Sandy?" asked Bob.

"Berlin at night. The searchlights and the flak, sir. Oh," he added feelingly, "I'm sure you'll enjoy it immensely."

"Yes, I'm sure we will," Bob replied doubtfully.

Wing Commander Cranbourne had no intention of missing such an important show as this, but although he was leading the three squadrons, the aircraft took off individually with no attempt to fly in formation in the air. This would be a long flight, for Berlin was almost three hundred miles beyond their previous objective.

"Hello, Turnip, hello, Turnip," called Don, for the code name of the station had been changed. " 'T' for Terrell calling, 'T' for Terrell calling. Are you receiving me, are you receiving me? Over to you, over to you."

Don went through the same familiar wireless checking routine while Bob carefully observed his instruments. All the aircraft had been flown a short time before the take-off. Carefully he checked the intercommunication system, for if he and Sandy could not exchange instructions, the trip would be a failure.

Impatiently, Bob waited for the green flash. Two squadrons already had taken off. Then his signal came, and he thrilled as always to the surge of power as the Stratohawk left the runway. The sky was completely overcast, so he climbed to get above it. Sandy would need the stars for his navigation tonight, for they would be flying over water for almost five hundred miles.

As they wheeled around on course, Don brought up the undercarriage and flaps. Higher and higher they climbed through the clouds. At twelve thousand feet they were on top, and Bob continued to the southeast, occasionally bearing one way or another according to directions from Sandy.

"There'll be no chance of seeing the coast line tonight, sir," said Sandy. "You might as well stick to this height if you've a mind to. If this kind of weather keeps up, I should hit it smack on the snoot."

By "snoot," Bob knew that Sandy meant the Elbe River, which would give them a definite course check on Berlin itself.

Don took over the controls and Bob leaned back, completely relaxed. Never had he seen a more beautiful night, or, as they say in Texas, a prettier night. They seemed to be flying over snowclad hills, for the moonlit clouds were white beneath them.

"Did you ever see anything more beautiful?" Bob asked Don.

"No, I don't think I ever have. Those clouds look as though you could really walk on them, don't they?"

There was little conversation on the trip, for the oxygen supply had to be conserved as much as possible.

"I think, sir," said Sandy, "that we'll be crossing the coast any time now."

"Perhaps we'd better go down for a check," suggested Bob.

"I don't think it will be necessary, sir."

Ahead of them great balls of fire were piercing the clouds and shooting high above them.

"That's what I meant, sir," said Sandy. "That will be Cuxhaven. Another aircraft stirred them up a bit. They can usually be counted on for a bearing, and as I'd expected, we've hit it right on the nose."

Now the flak was getting heavier. Bob, meanwhile, took avoiding action—changing his course, height, and direction of flight. By manipulating the throttles, he desynchronized the engines. He knew that ground locators were picking them up far below and would endeavor to set up a barrage ahead of them. Increasing his speed, he skirted widely to starboard as the most intensive anti-aircraft fire was concentrated on the port side and astern.

"I don't think you'll have any further trouble for awhile, sir," said Sandy, "unless it would be from enemy fighters."

But no enemy fighters appeared. Only two of their own aircraft. There were no lights in the cabin, but Sandy made frequent use of a small electric flashlight, or "torch," as he called it. In less than an hour now, they would be over the target.

Already the clouds were beginning to thin out and frequently Bob caught the reflection of a thin strip of water underneath.

"That will be the Elbe, sir," said Sandy, "and I'd advise you now to begin getting some height. We'll soon be over Hamburg and undoubtedly they'll have a nice little party planned for us."

The Elbe became a silvery slit as Bob climbed for altitude, but he knew that it was a wide river, narrowing out after it left the great port of Hamburg. In a few moments the city itself could be seen, naked in the face of the moonlight. At twenty thousand feet they were above the outskirts and the city took on the appearance of a huge jigsaw puzzle. Tiny pin pricks of light seemed to wink at them from beneath, and shells burst far below them. The next moment the shells were bursting directly ahead and again, quickly, Bob took avoiding action.

"They're shooting higher and higher all the time," said Sandy who, from his vantage point, could easily observe the scene below.

Climbing for more altitude, Bob avoided the barrage set up ahead and in a few moments they had passed the danger area. If the weather held, they should have no trouble. But there were clouds ahead and soon the river was blotted out.

"Just hold your course, sir," said Sandy reassuringly. "I can spot it through holes now and then."

Long since, while Don had been at the controls, Sandy had made the bombs live. Don and Bob were peering intently ahead.

"I think we've lost it, Bob," remarked Don.

"About ten miles back," emphasized Sandy, over the R.T. "That's as it should be, for the Elbe turned due south there. What is your course now, sir?"

Bob told him.

The Stratohawk was now headed almost due east, and on this bearing would pass well to the north of Berlin. That was not according to plan. The plan had been to follow the Havel River from its point of confluence with the Elbe.

"In this weather, sir," said Sandy, "I think the original plan would be too confusing. There are so many lakes and rivers mixed up down below that we might follow the wrong one. Keep going directly ahead and when we've passed Berlin we'll head south and hit the Spree River."

Bob had implicit confidence in Sandy's judgment,

and with an "O.K., Sandy," he held his course.
Anyone who could find that naval base last week
could find Berlin in this weather. Off to the right,
Bob could see anti-aircraft shells bursting among the
clouds and at infrequent intervals a searchlight burst
through. Some of the other aircraft were probably
over Berlin now.

Five minutes later Sandy directed, "O.K., sir, due
south. Now, sir, we should pick up the Spree in a
very few minutes—five at the most, but I'm afraid
you'll have to drop down."

Bob counted off the altitude as they went through
the clouds.

"All right, sir. Hold it, sir, that's enough."

Through the clouds Bob caught the glitter of the
small river, and banking hard to starboard, again
began to follow it in. The position of the target
and its relationship to other landmarks was photo-
graphed in Bob's mind. He knew that the River
Spree led into a canal and along the canal was the
huge aircraft engine works, their assigned target.
Planes of the first squadron had been carrying in-
cendiary bombs and Bob could now see the results
of their work. Fires were blazing over a wide area,

and in their light he could see the canal clearly.

"We'll have to come down, Sandy."

"Aye," agreed Sandy.

Searchlights were sweeping the sky and flak was rising in a steady brilliant stream.

"Five thousand, Sandy," called Bob, and down they went. "At any moment now that identifying intersecting canal should loom up."

"Left, left," called Sandy. He had seen the target.

In the light of near-by fires, Bob could see it also, and even as he looked, the roof began to blaze. Incendiaries had made direct hits. Holding his course, he waited for Sandy's instructions, but none came. He began to fear they would overshoot their target, when suddenly Sandy called, "Bombs gone." At just that moment the searchlights picked them up.

It seemed to Bob as though there were a hundred of them, and he could feel the whoosh-whoosh of shells as they tore by. The brilliance of the light flooded the plane inside and momentarily blinded him. Steeply he banked to starboard, and as he did so, there was a shattering crash. The Stratohawk had been hit.

The flash of the exploding shell had almost

blinded Don and Bob, and the acrid fumes were suffocating.

"Stand by to jump," ordered Bob.

Don quickly removed his parachute from the hooks above his head and clamped it on his chest, but the Stratohawk kept right on climbing. The engines seemed to be functioning perfectly. Bob had expected a sea of flame to engulf the greenhouse any moment.

"O.K., Sandy, it looks as if I were a little premature," said Bob.

"Aye," said Sandy, "but accidents are inevitable. Incidentally, sir," he added, "I had a fair view of the target as you came about, and I'm afraid the force of our explosion extinguished the fire started by the incendiaries."

The crackling in the intercom was terrific, and Bob barely could hear what Sandy said. "Good work, Sandy," he praised and made for the greater safety of the clouds. A moment later a shell seemed to burst almost beneath the Stratohawk's nose. "Are you all right, Sandy?" Bob called. There was no reply.

The flak still was coursing up at them but with decreasing intensity.

"Are you all right, Sandy?" Bob called again.

Now there was less crackling on the intercom system and Bob could hear a faint reply.

"Aye, sir," said Sandy, weakly. "Just a wee bit confused. One of those blasted oranges exploded almost in my face."

Bob leveled off at twenty thousand feet. Heading north he tried to return over their incoming course. The compass indicator was vibrating crazily. Now the sky was completely overcast and they were flying between two cloud layers.

"You'd better see what's wrong with Sandy, Don," advised Bob.

"Don't bother with me, sir," came back Sandy weakly. "I'm all right."

Don inched his way out of the seat and squeezed back into the navigator's shell. His hand found one of Sandy's feet and he pulled it gently, but there was no response from him. Don knew it was useless to shout over the roar of the engine. Groping in the dark, he found the little satchel in which the air observer kept his navigator's gear. Cold air was streaming by him as he flashed the light on Sandy's face. His eyes were closed but there was no sign of any injury.

"Sandy," shouted Don, almost in his ear. Still there was no response. Shining the light around, Don found a small jagged hole in the side wall. A flying piece of shell fragment st have hit Sandy, he decided. Reaching for his handkerchief, he tried to stop up the hole, but the space was too confined and he had to give up the attempt. He was beginning to feel a big groggy, for the air was thinning out in the navigator's shell.

Carefully he ran his hand over Sandy to discover any possible wounds, and he soon found from the jagged rent in his flying suit that the shell had struck Sandy in the hip. Don now tried to edge his way back out of the bombardier's shell. His heavy flying suit made this nearly impossible, but finally his toes caught a ledge and he was able to hoist himself the last few inches. Faint from lack of oxygen, he told Bob what had happened. Instantly sensing the situation, Bob nosed down to a lower level.

For awhile Don hung desperately to a guy rope

behind his seat, but in a few minutes he felt better.

"You'd better let me take over," he said to Bob, "and see what you can do for Sandy. I'm too big to get in there."

"Sure you're all right yourself?" asked Bob.

"I'm O.K. now."

"All right," said Bob quickly. "Hold her due northwest. Flak or no flak, we can't go up any higher."

Although it was now bitterly cold in the cabin, Bob took off his parachute, heavy life jacket, flying suit, and boots. Stowing them away behind the cockpit, he shoved himself forward to the navigator's shell. Slim as he was, it was a tight fit. Using the flashlight, he carefully examined Sandy's wound. It did not seem serious, although he was bleeding freely and his flying suit had been torn clear through and was soaked with blood. Taking a knife from Sandy's emergency kit, Bob cut away the suit from the wound and applied Monsel's solution to stop the flow of blood. He could feel Sandy's leg twitch when he touched the raw flesh. He looked at his face and saw that Sandy's eyes were now open and he was trying to speak.

Shoving forward, Bob shouted, "You'll be all right, fellow. Don't worry."

"You must turn off that torch, sir, and stick to your flying," said the navigator in a voice so weak that Bob could bare¹ distinguish the words even with his ear to Sandy's lips. "Northwest, sir," he added, "northwest."

Bob patted Sandy's shoulder reassuringly and looked again at the wound. The bleeding seemed to be lessening now. Taking a strip from Sandy's flying suit, Bob tried to stuff it into the hole in the wall of the plane. Finally it stuck, half outside and half in, and Bob jammed the satchel into the corner to divert the remaining draft. Most of the air was now cut off. Inching back out of the shell, Bob got his life jacket and gently tucked it around Sandy's head. Grimly he climbed back to his seat beside Don.

"How is he?" asked Don.

"I think he'll be all right," replied Bob, "if we can get him back soon."

"I've been bearing south a bit," said Don, "to avoid Hamburg. At this height we'd be dead ducks."

"Good idea," returned Bob. "I think we'll head

due west. Our best bet now is to get back to the nearest possible base."

"That's what I was thinking," agreed Don.

The space between the two cloud layers had now tightened up. Steadily they ploughed ahead through the clouds.

"Another hour," said Bob, "and we ought to make the coast."

"Just about," agreed Don.

Occasionally dim flashes of anti-aircraft fire broke the darkness around them.

"Someone's thinking about us, anyway," remarked Don after a long silence.

"Better take over again, Don, so I can see how Sandy's getting along."

Sandy's eyes were closed, but otherwise he seemed little changed. Carefully Bob uncovered the wound and found that the blood was still oozing out, but very slowly. He applied a little more Monsel's solution and returned to the cockpit.

"I think he'll make it all right, Don."

"I sure hope so," replied Don. "There aren't many like Sandy. By the way, when you go down again, Bob, give him this banana. I swiped it out of his bag when we were getting on board."

Checking his watch, Bob saw that it was almost an hour and a half since the raid on Berlin.

"We should be hitting the North Sea any time now," said Bob. "I think we'll drop down and have a look."

Slowly, so as not to disturb Sandy, they decreased their altitude, but they had to drop to a thousand feet before the clouds were left behind. Off to starboard there was a glare of flames.

"Blast furnaces," said Don.

"Yes, but we ought to be well out over the North Sea by now."

"I think we're bucking a fairly hefty wind."

Angry red eyes began to wink up from the ground beneath.

"And if we don't get out of here," surmised Bob, "we'll be bucking some nasty flak."

Banking gently off the course, Bob skirted the danger zone and then headed back on the course previously taken. Back in the clouds, they forged ahead for another fifteen minutes. It was now nearly five A.M. Dropping down again, they could see the ground, although faintly.

"There's something screwy about this." Bob was beginning to be alarmed. "There should be water beneath us, not land."

"That's right," agreed Don, "and furthermore do you notice that it's lighter ahead of us than it is behind?"

"Don't tell me we've been doing a 'wrong-way Corrigan' all this time!"

"Maybe I'm wrong," said Don. "Maybe over here the sun does rise in the west, but if you ask me, I think we've been going in the opposite direction."

"Well, if we are," said Bob, "there isn't much we can do about it now, for we don't have fuel enough to turn around and go back."

It was soon apparent that they had been heading directly east. Gradually, as the horizon began to lighten, the thin thread of a coast line materialized on their left.

"Well," said Bob after long thought, "we've got three choices."

"What are they?"

"We can try to make it home, or we can turn left for neutral Sweden, or we can land behind the Russian lines."

"There's really only one choice it seems to me," answered Don. "And that is Russia."

"Which means," went on Bob, "that we're flying smack over Germany right now, or occupied Poland or East Prussia or Lithuania, or something along that line. It might be discreet to get a little more altitude." He shoved the nose up.

The clouds were now lifting, too, almost as fast as the Stratohawk could climb. Soon the horizon was clearly defined and the ground beneath easily distinguished. Off to the left the coast line bore directly north, and as Bob turned to follow it, Don called out, "Aircraft below!"

Boosting the engines, Bob climbed quickly for the clouds. In a few minutes he ventured out cautiously, but now there was no sign of aircraft. The sea had disappeared and they were back on their due east course. On and on they flew over a wilderness of sparsely populated land, with no sign of aircraft in any direction.

Sandy's voice came up weakly through the intercom system, "How are you doing, sir? I must say this doesn't look like Scotland to me."

Bob told him what had happened. "The compasses and radio are out, Sandy, and the sun came up too late to help us."

"Well," replied Sandy philosophically, "I understand the Russians are a very friendly people, but I would suggest that we get well behind their lines."

"Could you stand some food, Sandy?" asked Bob.

"Aye," said Sandy, "I can always stand that."

Don took the controls and Bob wedged his way into the navigator's shell with Sandy's banana. Leaving his ration bag within Sandy's reach, he started back to the cockpit. At that moment the Stratohawk heeled violently. Grabbing a cross member, Bob hung on, unable to see what had happened. The plane then lurched sharply as Don poured out a short burst. Now he was climbing steeply, and Bob clung grimly to the cross member. He could dimly see Sandy, who was strapped tightly to the floor, calmly munching his banana. Still Don kept climbing, then banked sharply and flattened out. Bob scrambled back up into his seat and Don pointed to a ME 109 heading toward the ground. As Bob watched, it crashed in a mass of flames.

"There were two others," said Don calmly, "but they decided to leave."

"A bonnie bit of shooting," said Sandy over the intercom. "My congratulations to Mr. White."

"Sandy," called Don, "how are you doing?"

"I'm doing fine, sir, but whenever you have a bit more food, I'm sure it will speed my recovery."

"You're an old fake," Don teased, "and you'll get no more of my food."

Both Don and Bob were greatly relieved to know that Sandy was on his way back to normal.

"I've been doing some observing, sir," said Sandy, "and believe that if you'll hold this course, we ought to be behind their lines within the hour."

Bob also had been doing some figuring.

"Only last evening," went on Sandy, "I was studying the latest war maps on the eastern front. To the best of my recollection, the Russies have pushed the Jerries back in a semicircle between Leningrad and Moscow. Our best bet will be to head for that bulge, and I think, sir, if you'll bear slightly left, keeping the sun just a bit on the right, that we'll hit it fair and square."

Following this suggestion, Bob bore slightly to the left. Now it was necessary to keep beneath the clouds in order to see the sun.

"Keep your eyes peeled down there, Sandy," advised Bob, "and we'll do the same. We won't take on anything unless we have to."

The sun had now climbed well above the horizon, and it was a beautiful day. That is, it would have been a beautiful day if they had not been flying several hundred miles an hour in the wrong direction with a wounded navigator on board. The fuel gauge was now alarmingly near empty. They had carried an ample supply for the flight to Berlin and return, with an extra margin "just in case," but no allowance had been made for an excursion of this kind.

"Look, Bob," exclaimed Don excitedly.

Away to the left Bob saw a group of aircraft messing it up in the air. A regular dogfight was in progress, but the boys had no time or inclination to investigate it. This dogfight was their first indication that they were near the Russian line, for those planes were probably German and Russian aircraft.

"I think," said Sandy from below, "that we're coming close to the lines now. Yes," he went on, "I can see the German artillery quite clearly. At least, I can see artillery firing toward the east."

"If that's the case," said Bob, "we'd better get up in these clouds and go farther east before we drop down."

Five minutes later he advised, "Keep your eyes peeled, Sandy. We're dropping down."

Bob had no need for Sandy's help now. He himself could see open ranks of infantrymen approaching from the east across the fields. They jumped for cover as the plane flew toward them, apparently thinking it was a German aircraft. A few of them raised their rifles to fire as the plane approached, but dropped them at once when they saw the R.A.F. rondels under the wing tips.

"It looks as if we've arrived," said Bob. Almost as he spoke, puffs of smoke broke out around the advancing men.

"A line of tanks is moving in from the west, sir," Sandy reported.

Then ahead, to the right, Bob saw another line of tanks approaching in single file, coming from the east. He fervently hoped that he would not have to land right in the middle of a tank battle!

"I wish we could give the Russies some help," he said. "These cannon of ours might cause a little excitement." Although he did not say so, he expected the engines to fail at any moment for lack of fuel.

Sandy reported that the tanks were now spreading out and firing at each other.

In all directions the country looked perfectly flat, but Bob knew that it must be pitted with shell holes and hence a landing would be very dangerous. He and Don looked eagerly for anything that resembled an airfield, but there was none in sight. Climbing for more altitude, still hoping to spot a landing field, Bob heard the port engine cough and then die. Quickly he cut off the switch and full-feathered the propeller. His only guide for wind was the smoke from the artillery burst on the ground. He half banked to the right, which put him directly into the wind, then eased off on the starboard engine.

Ahead there were two groves of trees with a wide swath down the center that looked as if it had been cleared recently. Letting down the undercarriage and the flaps, Bob prepared to land. With only one engine he had no other choice, and even as he thought about it, the starboard engine died. With luck he'd make that strip which, now that he was nearer, was far wider than he had anticipated. He felt sorry for Sandy on the floor below, for the ground was rushing up fast. Then the wheels touched and they rode along, tail high. Finally the tail dropped and they jounced bumpily over the uneven ground.

Around the corner of the wood a tank came rushing toward them. Bob swerved sharply to the left in order to avoid striking it. Was it German or Russian? If German, they might soon be prisoners of war; if Russian, they might avoid that fate. Instinctively he reached to break the demolition switch covering.

The tank wheeled and began firing into the westerly woods. Not until then did Bob see the red star on the side. The plane had now rolled to a stop less than a hundred feet from the Russian tank. As the tank approached, a lid on the top was opened and a head appeared. Bob sighed thankfully when he saw the smile on the bearded face and the hand waving a friendly greeting.

Even as he spoke, explosive cannon shells were ripping up the ground in front of them. Just as suddenly the tank changed course, and frantically Bob tried to follow it through the cloud of dust caused by the shells. He felt sure that some of the shells must have struck the plane but he could see no evidence of damage.

Above the staccato barking of the tank's engine they could now hear the roaring of aircraft above them. It would come in a rising crescendo and then die out almost to nothingness.

Don's head was bent almost parallel with the cabin floor as he gazed upwards, mouth agape. "That," he shouted excitedly, "was a JU 87 diving on us with a Hurricane on his tail."

"A Hurricane!" repeated Bob. "You must be crazy. There aren't any Hurricanes around here."

"Oh, yes, there are," insisted Don. "And now I think there is one less JU 87." His head slowly came down to a normal angle.

Out of the corner of his eye Bob could see a flaming torch crash into the ground off to starboard and as he watched, fascinated, he saw the familiar silhouette of a Hawker Hurricane flash by.

"You're right, Don," admitted Bob happily. "That was a Hurricane. I saw the R.A.F. rondels. I remember now that there are some British fighter squadrons over here in Russia. What a break for us!"

"Aye," said Sandy, who hadn't spoken for some time. " 'Break' is the word. I saw the whole business. Yon Hurricane laddie jumped the Jerry before he could release his bombs."

"Well," said Bob as they finally rounded the corner of the woods, "nothing would surprise me now."

"That's what you think," replied Don who, glasses to eyes, was carefully scanning the terrain ahead. "If we find what I think we'll find, you'll be plenty surprised."

Bob watched the tank heading for a break in the woods, while the Stratohawk moved sluggishly along behind. Slowly but surely they neared the opening. A regular amphitheater had been cut in the side of the woods and the opening above had been camouflaged with green netting. Apparently materializing out of nowhere, aircraftmen in the uniform of the Royal Air Force took hold of the wings and helped guide the Stratohawk deeper into the woods. The towline was unfastened and the tank chugged around the plane and came to a halt.

In a daze, Bob and Don looked at each other.

"What do you make of it, Don?"

"You've got me." Don shook his head in bewilderment. "Excuse me while I look up that hot-dog stand."

Sandy had recovered sufficiently to wriggle his way out of the bombardier's nest by himself.

"You stay where you are, Sandy," said Bob authoritatively, "until I can get someone to help you."

Outside, Bob found Don in animated conversation with a young R.A.F. Flight Lieutenant.

"Welcome to Russia, Terrell," said the Flight Lieutenant. "My name is Weston. White has just told me how you happened to drop in and visit us. I must say that we'd just as soon you hadn't come, but now that you're here we'll try to make you comfortable."

"I have a wounded air observer who needs attention as quickly as possible." Bob decided that further explanations could wait. Sandy must be taken care of immediately.

At the command of the Flight Lieutenant an air-craftman ran off into the woods and in a few moments two orderlies appeared carrying a rolled-up stretcher. Gingerly they lowered Sandy through the Stratohawk's belly door His clothes were stained with blood, and his face was drawn and pale. Nevertheless there was a smile on his face as he weakly saluted Flight Lieutenant Weston.

"I have the reputation, sir," Sandy joked, "of being a reasonably good navigator, but this time I have amazed myself." And he grinned back at Don and Bob as they hurried him away on the stretcher.

"All right," said Weston. "Let's get out of here now."

"But what about the Stratohawk?" asked Bob. "Are we just going to leave her here?"

"That's all we can do right now, Terrell, and we'll hope it's enough protection. We'd better get underground, for the Jerries may be over here any minute."

The Flight Lieutenant led Don and Bob along the path taken by the stretcher-bearers. After walking about a quarter of a mile, they met a sentry pacing back and forth before an inclined door in a raised mound of earth. At a sign from Weston the sentry opened the door. The boys followed Weston down a flight of cement steps while the trap door closed behind them. As the door banged shut, a light flashed on, revealing another door in front of them. It opened as soon as they approached, and on passing through they found themselves in a long hallway.

"This is something like that Jerry base in France," said Bob.

"How's that?" asked Weston, who was leading the way along the hallway.

"Oh, don't mind Terrell," explained Don. "He divides his time between the Royal Air Force and the Luftwaffe." And before the astonished Weston could reply, Don told of Bob's escape from France in the stolen Messerschmitt several months before.

"It does sound as if you get around, Terrell," said Weston, grinning. "Here we are and make yourselves at home."

The boys found themselves in a sparsely furnished room. A long table and straight-backed chairs were lined up around the walls.

"This is the combination dispersal-mess-lounge room," explained Weston. "I'll get you fellows something to eat and the C.O. will be over in a minute to join us."

"Well," said Bob, "this whole business has got me beat."

"At least," rejoined Don, "there is food. That's the most important thing."

In a few minutes Weston returned, bringing with him Squadron Leader Simpson, Commanding Officer of the Hurricane Squadron.

"Glad to meet you chaps," heartily acknowledged Squadron Leader Simpson, "although I must say that up until a few minutes ago I was cussing you pretty roundly."

"How is that, sir?" inquired Don, as an orderly set down steaming mugs of coffee and plates of sandwiches.

"Why, because you unwittingly gave away our position," explained the Squadron Leader. "For almost a month now our Squadron has been operating out of four advanced bases similar to this. Landings are only made on signal when the sky is absolutely clear of hostile aircraft. You fellows blundered in today right under the nose of a JU 87. I think, though, that one of our boys got him before he could wireless our position."

"I'm certainly sorry, sir," replied Bob. "We hadn't the slightest idea."

"Of course you hadn't," agreed the C.O. "We know that. It's really a lucky thing for you that you landed where you did. We may be able to fix you so you can take off again."

"Really, sir?" A delighted smile broke out on Bob's face.

"We'll see," replied the C.O. "Tuck those sandwiches away and we'll look over that kite of yours. I'm anxious to see it anyway. By the way," he added, "the M.O. tells me that that navigator of yours had a pretty close shave but that he'll be all right in a fortnight. Right now he's weak from loss of blood."

Examination of the Stratohawk revealed that the wings had suffered some damage from anti-aircraft fire and that shell fragments had cut the wireless lines and, lodging behind the compass, had overcome the normal magnetic north and set it up in the opposite direction.

"So that's how you chaps got completely turned around," said the C.O. "I was wondering but didn't want to embarrass you by asking."

Bob then told him the story of the raid on Berlin and their early morning "wrong-way Corrigan" flight.

"That must have been a harrowing experience," said the C.O. "This sounds like a real airplane."

"It certainly is, sir," agreed Bob enthusiastically. He went on to tell something of its performance and ended with the simple statement, "There's nothing else like it."

"I suppose you're anxious to get back to Scotland," said the C.O.

Both Bob and Don agreed that they were. "We'd hate to leave without Sandy," added Don.

"How long will it take to make Flying Officer Terrell's aircraft serviceable?" Simpson asked the Flight Sergeant who had been examining Bob's plane.

"We can probably be finished with it by teatime, sir," replied the Flight Sergeant as matter-of-factly as though he were merely changing an automobile tire in a London garage.

"That's fine, sir," said the delighted Bob, "but how on earth . . ."

"I imagine you're curious as to how we do things here," chuckled the C.O. "Come along and I'll show you."

The boys walked along with the C.O., who was following behind the Stratohawk as it was dragged more deeply into the woods.

"You see," he explained, "we've had to depend a lot on nature, for the building of underground hangars is a terrific job. Now you can see for yourselves what I mean."

The Stratohawk had been hauled into a large enclosure beside several Hurricanes on which aircraftmen were busily working. Over the whole enclosure there was an arched roof some thirty feet above the floor. Brilliant droplights hung from the roof and Bob could hear the put-putting of a near-by motor which, he learned, was generating the electrical current. Amazement bordering on disbelief was clearly written on the boys' faces.

"That's something to figure out on the flight back home," suggested Squadron Leader Simpson. "A roof without walls that can't be seen by the enemy.

Now let's go see how the Sergeant is getting along."

Stowed comfortably away in his subterranean hospital bed, Sandy was doing very nicely. Empty dishes on a tray beside his cot testified to an undiminished appetite.

"Look at that," said Don. "It's disgusting the way that Scotsman eats. It's probably a good thing that we will be taking off without him."

Sandy, already pale, turned deathly white at these words.

"Without me, sir," he repeated, looking imploringly at Bob. "Why, I never felt better in my life. Oh, hello, doctor," he added weakly as the Medical Officer entered the room.

"Do you think that Sergeant McTavish will be able to take off with us tonight, Doctor?" asked Bob.

"Take off for where?" asked the Doctor.

"For our base in Scotland," replied Bob. "As a matter of fact I doubt if we can even find it without him."

"If it were anywhere else but Scotland I'd say he wouldn't make it," said the M.O. "But being a Scot myself, I know that the thought of that destination will be as fine as any medicine I can give him."

"Hurrah!" yelled Sandy.

At dinner that night Bob and Don met the rest of the pilots in the Hurricane Squadron, and also the Russian tank officer who had towed them in that morning. He spoke no English, so Weston, with his fluent Russian, acted as interpreter. Both Bob and Don thanked him warmly for his help, and in turn the Russian complimented Bob for his masterly handling of the Stratohawk in tow.

Both boys were somewhat chagrined, however, to hear from the Hurricane pilot who had shot down their morning attacker that his shells—and not those of the Junkers—had spewed the ground in front of them.

"You see, old chap," he apologized to Bob, "there was the blighter right beneath me and there were you right beneath the blighter, and someone had to get hurt. But," he added cheerfully, "now that I've met you, I'm awfully glad it wasn't you."

"So am I," agreed Bob feelingly.

CHAPTER XII

Bagging a Prize

At one a.m. Bob and Don said their good-byes to the pilots of the Hurricane Squadron, all of whom had stayed up to see them off. Bob knew that curiosity regarding the performance of the Stratohawk accounted for this unusual interest.

Sandy was tucked gently away in the bombardier's nest after the engines were warmed up under the hangar, but before the silenced Stratohawk was towed out to the broad clearing in front of the woods. Then to the accompaniment of a chorus of good wishes, Bob and Don climbed aboard. A tow bar rather than a tow rope had been attached to the plane, so there was now no danger of overrunning the towing tractor.

It was dark as pitch when Bob started the engines, then quickly poured in the power. There was no distinguishing the ground as they plunged forward, but in a moment they were climbing swiftly on a smooth, velvety incline. Their best way of returning the "Hurry-box" hospitality was to get away from there as quickly as possible, for even the pin pricks of exhaust flames in a take-off might give away the location to skilled enemy patrols.

The Hurricane C.O. had insisted on a wide petrol allowance, so they had nothing to worry about in regard to fuel. The fifteen-hundred mile jaunt ahead of them would carry them over Western Russia, Lithuania, East Prussia, and the Baltic Sea. Then skirting southern Sweden, they would make a bee-line over Denmark for the Scottish coast, with their first landfall nearly five hundred miles away.

If they had reckoned correctly, they should reach the coast by dawn. In the meantime, Bob took off in a generally northwest direction, climbing in order to shake off the overcast that was blacking out the stars.

"Looks like a high one," said Don.

"It certainly does," agreed Bob, glancing at the altimeter needle which already had stepped off twelve thousand feet. "I was in hopes that we could keep down in the lower stratos on Sandy's account."

"Never mind me, sir," said Sandy. "I'm as snug as a bug in a rug. Let's get up above yon scum so that I can get a reading."

"You'll be getting your reading soon, Sandy."

Almost as he spoke, the Stratohawk entered the cloud layer and for several minutes they breasted the moisture-laden atmosphere. Then as suddenly as they had entered that desolate area, they burst through into a veritable fairyland of twinkling diamonds and luminescent pearls.

"There you are, Sandy," called Don. "You may have your pick."

"I won't repeat that uncouth joke about the Irishman," answered Sandy, "who said he would rather have his shovel. I'll only need a few of these."

"Too bad," said Bob, while Sandy was taking his sights, "that we can't stay up here, but we'll have to conserve our oxygen."

It was nearly three hours later when Sandy estimated their position off Malmo, Sweden, and his estimate was almost immediately confirmed by the dim but widespread lights of Copenhagen.

"Nice shooting, Sandy," called out Don. "I suppose you realize I've been your pilot for the last hour. Wake up there," he called to the dozing Bob, "and see the pretty scenery. Incidentally, if you'll take over for awhile I'd like to eat some of that nice Russian lunch our Hurricane friends so thoughtfully provided."

"It was indeed thoughtful of those gentlemen to arrange it for us," cut in Sandy, accenting the *us*.

"You're supposed to be sick and to keep quiet," said Don, who had intended to switch off the intercom system before mentioning food.

"Take him some food," said Bob, laughing, "but let me have my share before you wolves get at it. Otherwise I'm apt to be the one who ends up starving."

The sky was quite clear now. There were no clouds either above or beneath. The contours of the Danish coast stood out plainly below. It was a perfect night for night fighters, but fortunately no hostile aircraft challenged them.

"This is beginning to get monotonous," said Don about an hour later as he relinquished the controls to Bob. "I'll certainly be glad when we get back to the base."

"That should be fairly soon now, sir," interjected Sandy over the intercom. "Unless I've miscalculated rather badly, we should be seeing Scotland any minute now."

Three pairs of eyes strained ahead through the early morning light for the first glimpse of the Scottish coast.

"I think I see it," called Don, "just a bit to starboard."

They had lost considerable altitude and the sea was now clearly visible beneath.

"Sorry, sir," corrected Sandy, "that's only some land fog rolling out, but the land won't be very far behind it."

Sandy was right, and a few minutes later they passed over the rugged coast line.

Don had been settling for another snooze, but now he suddenly awoke. "I can almost smell the coffee in the mess," he began to no one in particular. "What a morning this would be for flapjacks and country sausage."

Just as he was about to close his eyes in blissful anticipation they riveted on some distant specks against the sky. He nudged Bob and silently pointed to what he had discovered.

"Not so good," said Bob, switching off the R.T. "I can't understand why so many of our kites would be westbound at this hour of the morning."

"Just what I was thinking," agreed Don.

Although Sandy could not hear their conversation he could talk to them, and at that moment he seemed to divine their thoughts.

"I have been observing, sir," he announced to Bob, "a formation of aircraft at approximately twenty-five thousand feet dead ahead. It occurs to me that they might be enemy ships intent on bombing our base. Might I suggest that we lead them off on a false scent?"

"You're right, Sandy. That's a wonderful idea. Here goes."

"They're Jerries, all right," said Don quietly, lowering his powerful binoculars. "Twenty-four of the new high altitude Dornier bombers."

"Is that all?" mused Bob. "Keep a close eye on them, Don, for if they're after our secret base I want them to think they've had a real stroke of luck. In other words, I want them to follow us in."

"Now I get it," said Don. "You're heading for the dummy airdrome."

Bob nodded grimly. The Stratohawk was now ahead and below the Dorniers, fifteen thousand feet of air separating them from the formation. Bob knew that powerful glasses would be sweeping the landscape constantly and that any moment they would be spotted by the enemy.

"Watch 'em, Don," he warned. "I'm changing course to the north."

Neither pilot spoke while the Stratohawk banked sharply to starboard, but as Bob leveled off Don cried sharply, "They fell for it! They're following us!"

Ten minutes later the Stratohawk's landing wheels rolled on the soft turf at the fake airdrome. Bob came to a complete stop on one of the newly filled-in bomb craters, souvenir of a recent JU 87 visit.

"This ought to make a nice target for them," he said, referring to the darkly camouflaged Stratohawk standing on the fresh earth.

"You don't mean you're going to sit here?" asked the astonished Don.

"I am until I'm sure they think this is the airdrome," replied Bob.

"They're banking around for their run now, sir," said Sandy who, in spite of his silence, had been taking in the whole situation.

"In that case," said Bob, "it's high time for us to get out of here. Hang on," he yelled as the Stratohawk leaped for the sky. He knew that at any minute heavy demolition bombs would come hurtling down toward the area they had just left.

Now that the decoy game was over there was no further point in maintaining radio silence, and they would need some help soon. " 'T' for Terrell reporting," Bob called into the mouthpiece, "we are about to engage an enemy force at twenty-five thousand. . . ."

At that point Bob's message was interrupted by the terrific detonations from below. Huge sections of the hillside rose bodily into the air, while the Stratohawk wallowed about like a skiff in a heavy sea.

"That was about close enough," remarked Don. "Another ten seconds and our hair would have been full of heather."

As the Stratohawk bored upwards into the sky, Bob tried desperately to get through to the station. There was no response.

"We're either not getting through or they don't want to reply," he said. "Looks like we'll have to do this little job by ourselves."

The gap between the Dorniers and the Stratohawk

was now closing, and the Jerries were climbing fast in a compact formation. Lightened by releasing their bomb load, they had increased their speed, but instead of streaking for the distant clouds, they apparently were counting on their high ceiling to protect them.

Now the Stratohawk's altimeter was vibrating at thirty thousand feet. Only five thousand feet above, the Dorniers were still climbing. Slowing and surely the gap was closing, but if Bob went too close, the Dorniers' concentrated fire power would make short work of the Stratohawk's pressurized cabin. Gradually, always out of range, Bob maneuvered to the port side of the formation and, still climbing, rose beyond range above them. Too late the Dornier leader realized his intention, and as he dove for the greater safety of the clouds beneath, Bob tore down on the flock with cannon blazing. His shells created havoc with the tightly packed Dorniers as he roared across them in a diagonal line from rear to front. One plane, as it exploded in a mass of smoke and flame, enveloped two more plunging on from behind. Another plummeted toward the earth as smoke billowed forth from the starboard engine.

Still another, off to the left, slithered out of the formation and fell in lazy spirals toward the ground. Now the formation, or what was left of it, disappeared into the cloud bank beneath.

"That makes five, as I figure it," called the delighted Sandy.

"Good heavens," replied Bob, "I'd forgotten about you, Sandy. Are you all right?"

"Dinna fret aboot me, lad," replied Sandy who, in the excitement, broke into Scottish dialect. "See if ye canna make it a roond half-dozen."

"Want to take over, Don?" inquired Bob as he skirted the heaviest cloud mass and dove to get under them.

"You're doing all right for my money," Don replied, grinning. "Lead on, Macduff."

When they reached the bottom of the cloud layer one lone Dornier was haring off for the coast.

"There's your sixth, sir," called Sandy.

As Bob moved in for the kill, he noted that something was wrong. One of the Dornier's engines was throwing out great blobs of smoke.

"Here come the Stratohawks," called Don. "They got our message after all."

"Good," replied Bob, "while they're taking care of the rest, maybe we can get this fellow home."

Pressing the button, Bob spewed a short burst into the Dornier's port wing tip. The results were immediate. Bits of metal were chipped off into the air and the wing came up as the plane banked desperately to starboard. As he dove, the tail gunner let off a defiant burst at the Stratohawk, but it passed by harmlessly. Seeing the Dornier try to turn back toward sea, Bob let him have another burst in the wing tip. There was no fire from the tail gunner this time. He had received his orders.

Bob pulled around ahead of the Dornier and dove toward the ground. Sluggishly the larger aircraft tried to follow. In a few more minutes Bob led them into the real runway and then circled threateningly behind. When the Dornier had rolled to a stop, Bob brought the Stratohawk in just behind, guns full on the long Nazi aircraft. As Don leaped from the Stratohawk, service revolver in hand, the crew descended from the Dornier, hands aloft.

Bob waited in the Stratohawk while Don examined the Dornier's engine and relieved the crew of their weapons. Then, bringing their revolvers over to the Stratohawk, Don sang out that he'd taxi the Dornier in ahead of him.

"O.K.," agreed Bob. "I'll be right behind you."

The Flight Sergeant's eyes were almost popping out of his head when the Dornier rolled up on the tarmac.

"We'd given you up, Mr. Terrell," he greeted Bob, as the latter clambered stiffly from the Stratohawk.

"Here we are, anyway, with guests," added Bob. "Hurry up a stretcher, will you, Flight, Sergeant McTavish has been wounded."

The dispersal hut was practically empty when Don and Bob reached there with their prisoners. Squadron Leader Anderson greeted them as they came in the door.

"Apparently anything can happen in this war," he said. "We'd written you chaps off the books twenty-four hours ago, and now you come back with company."

"I hope we won't be putting you out, sir," said Bob in mock apology, "but Mr. White and Sergeant Mc-Tavish and I thought you might be interested in seeing one of those new high altitude Dorniers."

"No," said Anderson, "you don't mean . . . you haven't!"

"I do mean," replied Bob, "and what's more it's parked down there on B tarmac right now. All intact except for a few chips off the port wing."

Hurriedly the Squadron Leader wrung Bob's hand, then rushed down to the hangar.

"I wish that people wouldn't seem so surprised at our being back," said Bob. "It sort of sounds as if they could get along without us easily enough."

"I'm afraid we're going to have to, whether we like the idea or not," said Wing Commander Cranbourne who had slipped in quietly through the dispersal door behind them.

"Hello, sir," said Bob and Don together.

"Come on in to my office where we can talk," replied the Commanding Officer. "We knew, of course, that you were somewhere in the neighborhood when we received that interrupted wireless message earlier this morning. Then a few moments ago I learned from Squadron Leader Anderson that you'd arrived. I might add that he was most enthusiastic about the present you brought him. Now tell me about yourselves."

While the Commanding Officer listened intently, Bob told of their adventures following the raid on Berlin up to the capturing of the Dornier bomber.

"There's only one important point Terrell failed to mention," added Don.

"Do you mean about shooting down the five Dorniers?" asked the C.O.

"Yes, I do, sir," said the surprised Don.

"I've heard all about that from Sandy who, by the way, will be up and around in a few days, according to the M.O. I won't say any more now, except that you've all done a fine job. After dinner I'll have an important announcement to make."

The afternoon dragged interminably for the boys until Eric Prentiss and Roy Benson returned from a daylight raid. Then there was plenty of news to catch up on.

At the end of dinner the C.O. pushed back his chair, and conversation ceased as he rose to his feet. "Gentlemen," he began, "I have a surprise for all of you. It's about one of your number who has unex-

pectedly returned but who will be leaving us very
soon." As he said this, all eyes turned toward Don
and Bob. "No," went on the C.O., "I'm not going to
talk about that inadvertent trip to Russia made by
Mr. Terrell and Mr. White, together with Sergeant
McTavish." Here the C.O. was interrupted by loud
laughter, for apparently the story had been circu-
lated. "And I'm not going to discuss their amazing
victories over the Dorniers this morning, which incidentally was one of the greatest shows I've ever
witnessed, nor their capturing intact the high altitude Dornier bomber. No, what I have to tell you
is about an incident that happened some time back
when, on my orders, Flying Officer Terrell was relieved from flying duty while most of the rest of us
went off on a raid over Norway. What Flying Officer Terrell did at that time saved most of us either
from losing our lives or becoming prisoners of war."
Then the C.O. went on to tell about the switches.
When he had finished, a great cheer went up for
Bob.

"I'm not quite through," continued the C.O. "I'm
able to tell you all this because today we found the
culprits who were responsible for the installation of

these switches at the factory, and I am thankful to say they have confessed and no one at this station is involved.

"Now for the sad news. Terrell will be ing us and with him will go all the American pilots on the station. In addition will go Flying Officer Eric Prentiss and Pilot Officer Don White. Also certain air observers, among them," he added smilingly to Bob, "a certain Sergeant McTavish, who swears he knows the Far East like the back of his hand."

Now bedlam really broke loose in the mess. There was no longer any doubt about where they would be headed. Bob Terrell knew that he soon would be at grips with the treacherous Japs.

THE END